Losing Ground

Losing Ground

CATHERINE AIRD

Allison & Busby Limited
13 Charlotte Mews
London W1T 4EJ
www.allisonandbusby.com

Hardcover published in Great Britain in 2007.
This paperback edition published in 2008.

A CIP catalogue record for this book is available from
the British Library.

10 9 8 7 6 5 4 3 2 1

ISBN 978-0-7490-7962-8

The paper used for this Allison & Busby publication
has been produced from trees that have been legally sourced
from well-managed and credibly certified forests.

Printed and bound in the UK by
CPI Bookmarque, Croydon, CR0 4TD

CATHERINE AIRD is the author of more than twenty crime novels and story collections, most of which feature Detective Chief Inspector CD Sloan. She holds an honorary MA from the University of Kent and was made an MBE. Her other works include *Hole in One*, *Amendment of Life* and *Little Knell*. Apart from writing the successful *Chronicles Of Calleshire* she has also written and edited a series of village histories and is active in village life. She lives in England.

For Peach, Plum and Henry
with love

CHAPTER ONE

'There's something I want, Stu,' said Jason Burke, indicating a piece of paper he'd just tossed on the table in front of Stuart Bellamy. 'Get a load of that.'

Bellamy picked up the paper and read out slowly, 'A view of Tolmie Park near the market town of Berebury photographed from the air.'

'That's right.' Burke strummed a few notes on a guitar. 'It's over Calleford way.'

Bellamy peered at the picture more closely and said warily, 'Jason, this is a picture of a socking big country house in the middle of a large park.'

'That's right.' Jason bent more carefully over the guitar and twanged the same notes over again. And again. 'It's in the middle of nowhere, actually.'

'A country house that looks as if it's falling down,' pointed out Bellamy.

'It does, doesn't it?' agreed Jason, reaching for a sheet of music. 'I expect it is, too. It's pretty old.'

'It looks it,' said Bellamy, adding studiously, 'Jason, you've got a house already. A nice one.'

'Sure,' said Jason agreeably, 'but I want this one, too.'

Stuart Bellamy said nothing for a moment. Working as the

manager of Jason Burke, who was known to the wider world of Pop Music as Kevin Cowlick, had already led him into the wilder areas of finance – ones that had not been covered by his own accountancy apprenticeship. Actually, Bellamy hadn't completed his apprenticeship to become a fully qualified accountant – not that Jason cared about that – but every now and then he wished he had. This was one of those times.

Eventually, sounding as if he understood his employer's way of thought, he said, 'Of course, it's bigger than this one you've got now.' He waved towards the forty-track synthesiser at the other end of the room. 'And there'd be much more room for extra equipment.'

'Oh, it's not that,' said Jason casually, his hand straying to the lock of hair that fell across his forehead and was the inspiration for his stage name. 'It's for sentimental reasons. That's why I want it.'

'Ah…' murmured Stuart Bellamy.

'First big bike ride me and my mate took out of Luston – we were only nippers at the time – we fetched up at this Tolmie Park and I thought that if I got to be rich and famous that I'd like to live there.'

'I see,' said Bellamy. And he did. Jason was not the only young man to have spotted a goal early in life and used it as something to aim for or to lay at the feet of some lady. The difference was that Jason was still young…and so far there was no lady.

'And now I'm rich and famous,' said Jason simply, 'I'm going to have it.' He resumed playing his guitar.

'That may be easier said than done,' pointed out Bellamy cautiously. 'Whoever owns it may not want to sell.'

'Every man has his price,' responded Jason. This was one thing that success and its consequent great wealth had already taught the young pop star.

'True,' said Stuart Bellamy, 'very true, but don't forget it may cost.'

Jason Burke let his glance travel meaningfully over a rack of albums all with the name of Kevin Cowlick on them before he said again 'I want it.'

'Sure,' said Bellamy.

'So go get it for me, Stu – oh, and Stu...'

'Yes?'

'Get me another djembe, too.'

'Okey dokey.' Stuart Bellamy thought how like Jason it was to want him to buy for him both a vast country estate and a new drum in the same breath. 'Will do.'

'It's an outrage,' spluttered Marcus Fixby-Smith, curator of the Greatorex Museum in Granary Row, Berebury. 'An absolute outrage.'

'It would appear to be a case of theft,' pronounced Detective Inspector CD Sloan, rather less emotionally. He was head of the tiny Criminal Investigation Department of F Division of the Calleshire County Constabulary. As such almost all matters that could not be diverted to Traffic Division or the Family Case Officer landed up on his plate.

This was one of them.

'Robbery with violence,' insisted the curator, pointing to the damaged glass top of a showcase.

'Breaking and entering,' countered Sloan briskly, indicating the smashed window of the gallery and broken glass.

The museum curator tossed his long hair out of his eyes and said, 'Inspector, the thief, whoever he was, as well as stealing a portrait, did violence to this show cabinet and quite possibly to the exhibition pieces on display inside it.'

'I can see that that is very likely, sir,' agreed Sloan, peering at the damaged piece of museum furniture and its disarranged contents.

'He must have gone through the glass top while he was standing on it to reach up to get at the portrait,' declared Fixby-Smith.

'You could well be right about that,' said Sloan equably. 'Where would this showcase have been standing in the ordinary way?'

Marcus Fixby-Smith waved a hand and pointed to the middle of the room. 'Just over there. Easy enough to drag it up against the wall and hop onto it.'

The museum curator had at his side his assistant, an intelligent and able young woman wearing glasses, called Hilary Collins. Her low-key sandy-coloured blouse and skirt were in direct contrast to the flamboyant clothes of her boss.

Detective Inspector CD Sloan, known to his friends in the Force for obvious reasons as 'Seedy', had not been quite so fortunate. He had with him at his side at the museum as his assistant Detective Constable Crosby, dressed – at least in theory – in what was officially described in police circles as plain clothes.

Crosby, though admittedly young, was not really up to being at the cutting edge of detection. What Superintendent Leeyes had said when the call from the museum had come through was: 'Take him with you, Sloan. He can't do any more damage there and he might even learn something.'

Seeing the constable advancing at the double on the broken glass of the show cabinet now, Sloan wasn't so sure of either the premise or the possibility. 'The Scenes of Crime Officer will want to examine that first, Crosby,' he said swiftly, motioning him back.

All four of them were standing immediately under the place on the wall of the museum where, until recently, had hung the portrait of Sir Francis Edward Petherton Filligree, 4th Baronet, of Tolmie Park, near Berebury. The oil painting had been cut neatly from its ornate gilt frame. Along the lower edge of the frame was inscribed in black letters the subject's name and dates. Above this now in the place of the portrait was just an old wooden backing board.

Detective Inspector Sloan turned over a new page in his notebook and wrote down the place, date and time. 'Would this have been a particularly valuable painting, sir?'

The curator threw out his chest. 'We have many more important pieces here in the museum naturally, but any portrait by Peter de Vesey has its own value.'

'Who he?' asked Detective Constable Crosby insouciantly.

Marcus Fixby-Smith favoured him with the pained expression of an expert talking to a total ignoramus. 'A well-known local artist, very popular with the eighteenth-century landed classes of Calleshire.'

'He painted most of them in his day,' put in Hilary Collins helpfully. 'We've got several more works by the same artist in our collection here and there are some others over in the Calleshire museum and Art Gallery.'

'We have the best ones, though,' put in Fixby-Smith quickly.

Sloan, who could recognise a turf war as well as the next man, tried another tack. 'Would you care to put a value on what has been stolen?'

'Impossible,' declared Fixby-Smith histrionically.

'Not easy,' explained Hilary Collins. 'De Vesey portraits so seldom come on the market these days. Families that have them do like to hang onto them, you know.'

'Ancestor-worship,' said Detective Constable Crosby under his breath.

'So why haven't the Filligrees still got Sir Francis?' enquired Sloan mildly.

'I think it could just be because there aren't any of them left. Filligrees, I mean,' said Hilary Collins. 'But I don't know that for sure.'

'Perhaps they were broke and had to flog him off,' put in Crosby. 'Like selling the family silver.'

The museum curator grimaced. 'Worse, we might even have been given him. Then we'd have had to have him – I mean, it – whether we liked it or not.' Since this didn't quite accord with his earlier stance he added hastily. 'Of course, we're always pleased to have anything by Peter de Vesey. Naturally.'

More practically, Hilary Collins said, 'I turned up our Accession List before you arrived, Inspector, and it looks as if the portrait came into our collection at some time in the late nineteen-thirties. We have it in our records as having got it on long term loan from the family.'

'There would have been very little market for this sort of work just before the war,' put in the museum curator authoritatively. 'Things were very flat in that field then.'

'They were hard times,' said Sloan, who had his

grandparents' memories of those years to go on.

'And I believe the Army requisitioned the house in the war...' said Hilary Collins.

'Harder times still,' said Sloan. That he'd learnt from his own parents.

'Then after the war,' she resumed, 'I understand the authorities used it for a while to house delinquent children...'

It would be a toss-up, thought Sloan, whether they would have done more or less damage than the rough soldiery. 'And then?' he asked.

'I have an idea that at one time someone wanted to carve the place up into self-contained flats but keeping the façade and the style,' replied Hilary Collins. 'That was after the delinquent children.'

'You know the sort of thing, Inspector,' the curator interrupted her, 'grand country house living without having to worry about the roof or the drive all on your own.'

'I do,' said Sloan. They knew all about the aspirational society in the criminal investigation world, too.

'Delusions of grandeur, if you ask me,' muttered Crosby.

'And then there was a rumour about having a golf course there.' Hilary Collins frowned. 'I rather think something went wrong with a bank loan at that stage but that was only hearsay. I'm not sure.'

'So?' asked Sloan, mindful of more important problems than a break-in and the history of an old building awaiting him back at the police station. Bank loans that had gone wrong were not exactly hot news there either.

'I expect the planning people wouldn't wear any development,' said Fixby-Smith. 'Listed building status and all that. All they ever want is for everything to stay "as is". Still do.'

'Then?' asked Sloan patiently.

Hilary Collins screwed up her eyes in the effort of recollection. 'After that I think it was empty for a long while – got thoroughly neglected. The damp got in and then wet rot.'

'Disgraceful,' said Fixby-Smith automatically.

'I have an idea the local council tried to serve repair notices on the owners but they couldn't find them.'

'Neither could the bank, I expect,' put in Crosby.

'No responsibility, some people,' said Fixby-Smith.

'No money, more like,' offered Detective Constable Crosby, who lived nearer the ground.

'I heard that a rather dodgy printing firm moved in after that,' said Hilary Collins steadily. 'They put one of their heavy presses in the old billiard room – that sort of thing but who they paid their rent to, I couldn't say.'

'If they did,' said Crosby.

The curator gave a snort and said, 'Disgraceful, when you come to think about it. Pure sacrilege.'

'Needs must,' contributed Crosby. 'Or the march of progress or something.'

Fixby-Smith looked at the detective constable as if he was seeing him for the first time. 'I may say that if that's what you are pleased to call progress, Constable, then...'

'Sir,' Detective Inspector Sloan interrupted him swiftly, turning away from the blank space on the wall where the portrait had been and pointing instead at the damaged display cabinet below it. 'Do you know what will have been in that?'

The curator frowned. 'Anglo-Saxon artefacts, I think. That right, Hilary?'

'Yes, Mr Fixby-Smith. Local ones from the site near Larking. Part of the Professor Michael Ripley bequest.' She advanced on the display case and peered in. 'I know there was a bronze shield in it – yes, that's still here. I'd have to check the other items in our records to see if anything is missing.'

'That's the Dark Ages, isn't it?' said Detective Constable Crosby chattily. 'The Anglo-Saxons, I mean.'

The curator immediately launched into hortative mode. 'Calleshire was quite an important place in post-Roman times. There was a big Anglo-Saxon settlement over Larking way and another one near Almstone, both excavated by the late Professor Michael Ripley, a well-known local archaeologist.' He waved an arm. 'There is some suggestion that the name relates to the re-use by the Anglo-Saxons of Roman stone there beside the river Alm.'

'Waste not, want not,' observed Detective Constable Crosby to no one in particular.

Detective Inspector Sloan who, among other problems, had a complicated case of transactional fraud on his hands back at the police station, returned to the matter in hand. 'As you will know, sir,' he said to the curator, 'there are well-established mechanisms for informing the art world of thefts such as these...'

'Yes, yes,' Marcus Fixby-Smith interrupted him testily, 'the Art Loss Register, but I want that portrait back and I also want to know why it has been stolen.'

'So do we,' Sloan reassured him. Actually the police priority was to find out who it was who had done the stealing and then charge him – or sometimes, but not often, her – with burglary but he saw no reason to say so. His own priority just now was to get back to work on the more pressing matters awaiting him back at the police station.

Marcus Fixby-Smith tossed his flowing mane back like an irate horse. 'Even so, Inspector…'

'And this means, sir,' he said firmly, 'that you will have to keep this gallery closed for the time being.'

Hilary Collins nodded intelligently while the curator snapped, 'How long for exactly?'

'Until our enquiries are complete,' responded Detective Inspector Sloan smoothly, silently acknowledging to himself that well-worn formulae did have their uses. 'May I take it that this was just a straightforward portrait?'

'Typical painting of the period,' the curator came back promptly. 'Portrait of Sir Francis Filligree leaning against a tree near the house, his new wife at his side, with a distant view of the village church at Tolmie in the background and some lobster shells at his feet.'

'Lobster shells?' said Sloan. Kinnisport and the sea were quite a distance away from Tolmie.

'Lobster and crab shells, actually,' Hilary Collins made the correction diffidently. 'I believe there are similar shells in the Filligree coat of arms, too.'

'In his day,' explained the curator, 'Sir Francis was a member of a group of young rabble-rousers called the Crustaceans.'

'A sort of Hellfire Club, I'm afraid,' supplemented Hilary Collins.

'So what's new?' observed Detective Constable Crosby,

victim of several Saturday night fights with the young and drunk with nothing else to do.

Hilary Collins coughed. 'I rather think that there was also a particularly good view of Tolmie Park in the upper left hand corner of the painting.'

'That's what I said,' trumpeted Marcus Fixby-Smith. 'Absolutely typical for its time. Think Thomas Gainsborough's famous painting of "Mr and Mrs Robert Andrews"…'

'Who they?' asked Detective Constable Crosby predictably.

'A nouveau riche couple – he married money – wanting the world to know how well they'd done,' said Fixby-Smith.

'There's a lot of that about,' said Crosby.

Not as much, thought Sloan to himself, if the Proceeds of Crime Act got to them first. He had high hopes of this new piece of legislation – and the Assets Recovery Agency – succeeding with the fraud case he was working on now. When he could get to it, that is.

'In 1748 in the case of the Andrews,' added Fixby-Smith, pedantically. 'I'm not sure offhand of the date of Peter de Vesey's portrait of Sir Francis Filligree.'

'Nothing changes, anyway,' said Crosby, patently unimpressed.

Hilary Collins kept her gaze on the damaged door to the gallery. 'I believe the view of the house in the painting was thought to be an unusual one. We will have a photograph of it in our records – I'll look it out for you, Inspector.'

Detective Inspector Sloan looked up alertly. 'Unusual?'

'As Mr Fixby-Smith has pointed out,' she said with careful loyalty, 'it was – I mean, is – typical for its time but I see from their notes that there was something our predecessors here in the museum found noteworthy when they accessed it all those years ago…'

Detective Inspector Sloan listened with attention as Hilary Collins balanced the difficult tightrope between tact and toadying. The curator obviously hadn't found anything interesting about the portrait at all.

'It was the particular view of the house,' she said. 'Apparently Tolmie Park couldn't be seen in the ordinary way later – certainly not in our time – from the aspect in the painting.' Unlike that of the curator, Hilary Collins' mouse-coloured hair didn't need tossing about to make a point. 'Not afterwards.'

'Afterwards?' queried Sloan.

'After some subsequent improvements by Humphry Repton,' she said.

'And the Victorians,' snapped the curator. 'Mustn't forget them. If they could ever be said to have improved anything.'

'Later drawings and photographs always show the front of the house flat on,' persisted Hilary Collins in a detached way.

'Full frontal,' murmured Detective Constable Crosby almost – but not quite – inaudibly.

'And the view in the portrait?' asked Sloan swiftly. Informality might be the watchword for today's policing but it could go too far.

'If my memory is right, Inspector,' said Hilary Collins, primly ignoring the detective constable's observation, 'that showed the house as seen from the south-east as it was in the beginning.'

'Before Humphry Repton got his hands on the landscape.'

The curator reasserted himself with practised ease. 'There should be one of his little red books about it here in the museum somewhere.'

'Really, sir?' The only little red book that Sloan knew about had political rather than architectural connections but all information was grist to the police mill. He tucked the fact away in the back of his mind. 'Now, about your alarm system here…'

Hilary Collins waved a hand in the direction of the window but before they could get near enough to look at it Detective Inspector Sloan's personal mobile telephone started to ring.

It was Superintendent Leeyes from the police station at Berebury on the other end of the line. 'Get yourselves over to Tolmie Park as quickly as you can, Sloan,' he commanded. 'The house there is on fire.'

CHAPTER TWO

Somewhere where they most definitely did think of change as progress was at the firm of Berebury Homes Ltd. The local development and construction company had its offices in Berebury's business quarter down by the river. A Project Team meeting was in progress there now.

There were four people present. One of them, Robert Selby, their financial controller, was in full voice. As was usual with those of that ilk, the money man was downplaying anything in the nature of good news. Since the others there knew only too well of Selby's infinite capacity to cast a decided blight on any proceedings involving money, the downside of what he had to say was accordingly discounted by them all.

'So the finance for the Tolmie Park development project is now at an important juncture...' Selby was saying, tapping the notes on the table in front of him for greater emphasis, when he was interrupted by the arrival of Lionel Perry, Chairman and Managing Director of Berebury Homes, Ltd.

'Sorry to be late, everybody,' Perry said breezily, slipping into the empty chair at the top of the table. Hung on the wall behind him was a photograph of Mont Blanc, the Swiss mountain. 'Puncture. Haven't had one for ages. Do carry on Robert. You were saying something about Tolmie Park, I think...'

'Yes, Lionel,' lumbered on Robert Selby ponderously, 'I was just about to point out that the development there is only going to come right financially if we get planning permission for the whole area from the word go to do it our way.' He looked round at them all. 'I hope that you all realise that. Otherwise…'

'I'm sure they do,' said Lionel Perry. He glanced round with a quick complicit smile at all the others. 'That's very important.'

'And getting planning permission itself costs a lot as well,' continued Robert Selby, his pencil still beating a steady tattoo on the outside of his file. Like the chairman, he was dressed in a sober business suit. On the wall behind him was a photograph of the Jungfrau.

'Bean counter,' whispered Derek Hitchin, their project manager.

Selby, who hadn't heard him, carried on. 'I've got my people working on some additional figures now but as you know Section 106 agreements are no help to man nor beast.'

'Would someone please have the goodness to explain to me what a Section 106 agreement is?' Auriole Allen was the only woman present at the meeting and didn't pretend to be knowledgeable about building development, only about advertising and public relations. The photograph behind her chair was of the Silberhorn bathed in the evening Alpenglow.

'Legally binding agreements between local authorities and developers and landowners,' spelt out Robert Selby.

She looked bewildered. 'But we own the land at Tolmie and we're also the developers of it, aren't we?'

'Too right, we are,' said Selby sourly. 'That means it's just us and them.'

'I don't think any of us need any reminding of the initial costs, Robert,' intervened Perry, effortlessly resuming the lead. 'It's not new. It happens every time we start talking about a major development project like this.'

He might not have spoken, so quickly did Selby go back to his theme. 'And quite apart from the application charges, Lionel, there's what Berebury Council are going to sting us for in the way of all the new roads they'll want putting in,' he persisted. 'Let alone roundabouts.'

'Require us to put in, you mean,' said Derek Hitchin, giving a little snort. He was a short peppery man and the mud-spattered donkey-jacket he affected was as much a statement as what he was saying. The photograph on the wall behind his chair was as craggy as his personality: the north face of the Eiger. 'At least they're not charging us for planning gain any more.'

'But you all know that roundabouts cost a bomb, too,' said Robert Selby, reasserting his role as the finance man. 'You're talking big money there.'

'They'll want one of those where our land meets the road to the village.' Derek Hitchin banged the pile of papers on the table in front of him and said sharply, 'Bound to. We all know that the existing entrance won't do, coming out on a blind corner like it does. May I point out, too, Lionel, that straightforward outline planning permission is not the only thing that this Tolmie Park undertaking is dependent on. Don't forget that the final planning footprint isn't even fixed yet.'

'Go on,' said Lionel Perry, stealing a surreptitious glance at his wristwatch. He was due on the first tee of Berebury Golf Course in exactly ninety minutes' time but had no intention of saying so.

'And if we don't get enabling permission for the land beyond the ditch...' resumed Hitchin.

'The ha-ha, if you don't mind,' put in a man called Randolph Mansfield in a pained voice. He was an architect and had never taken to wearing a collar and tie. He did, though, favour shaggy pale blue denim trousers that he thought made him look younger than he was and really with it. 'It's called a ha-ha, not a ditch and it's designed to make gardens look bigger while keeping the livestock out.'

Derek Hitchin pointedly ignored him, going on, 'As I was saying, we must get planning permission for all the land beyond the ditch, outside the village envelope or not. We need it to make the project viable. Every bit of it.'

'The Muster Green, you mean,' put in the chairman, demonstrating how conversant he was with the matter in hand.

'If we don't get planning permission for the Muster Green on top of the go-ahead for the rest of the parkland then we won't be able to do anything with the old heap because we won't have enough decent access to satisfy the Highways people and that's that,' finished Derek Hitchin flatly. 'Knockdown bargain or not.'

Auriole Allen stirred uneasily and said, 'Derek, as the person in charge of press and public relations in this firm, might I point out that it would be as well if we avoided referring to Tolmie Park...'

'What's left of it,' interrupted Derek Hitchin, quite unrepentant.

'What's left of it, then,' conceded Auriole Allen, 'as an old heap.'

It was house policy to keep the belligerent Derek Hitchin, their very able but distinctly short-fused project manager, away from as many outside contacts as possible. His abrasive manner worked very well with sub-contractors and suppliers; it went down less well with officials and local councillors.

And the press. Especially the press.

Auriole Allen turned on a winning professional smile and went on, 'The local papers might get to hear of it and you know what they're like when they sense a row. And then before you can say knife, it's in all the nationals.'

'Auriole's right, of course,' said Lionel Perry peaceably, well aware that there was nothing the combative Hitchin liked better than a row.

With anyone. With everyone.

'Not a good idea, Derek,' he went on easily. Lionel Perry was the very embodiment of a company chairman. Silver-haired and silver-tongued, and of a notably benevolent mien, he photographed well and knew it. It was Lionel Perry's face that figured on the firm's advertisements and promotional brochures. It was an image that was worth a lot.

'Don't forget, Derek, that the history of the bank's involvement in Tolmie Park has been kept out of the papers.'

'So far,' Auriole Allen reminded them tautly. 'Only so far. Don't forget that you can never be quite sure what the press know but aren't going to print until the time's ripe. They're very good at that.'

'The Calleshire and Counties Bank won't thank us for making it public anyway,' said the chairman.

Robert Selby sniffed. 'Too right, they won't. Their Douglas Anderson has always been a bit tight-lipped about what happened there.'

Lionel Perry added lightly, 'And you never know when we're going to need some extra finance from them ourselves.'

'Worse than the press,' Robert Selby came back smartly in his customary role as Cassandra, 'is that the Berebury Council's conservation people might get to hear that Derek here thinks the house an old heap. You know what they're like with their precious listed buildings.'

'You don't have to tell me,' grumbled Randolph Mansfield. 'They behave as if every single old building in the county of Calleshire belonged to them.' Even though strictly speaking he was the firm's architect, Mansfield was still a man with his own ideas about what should be done with all buildings – old and new.

'But they talk about them as if they're ours all right whenever hard cash comes into it,' snapped the finance director. 'They're not theirs then. Oh, dear me, no. When it comes to paying anything out, then they're ours.'

'Ours? I ask you!' spluttered Derek Hitchin, 'when they won't let you lay a single finger on them without their permission. Ours, indeed!'

'Which in the broadest sense,' said the chairman calmly, 'I suppose they are, since we all live in Calleshire and enjoy them.'

Of all those present only Auriole Allen appreciated the public relations value of this anodyne statement. The others ignored it for the guff it was.

Lionel Perry stroked his chin and said sagely, 'This Muster Green you're talking about – I suppose if the worst comes to the worst and we can't get planning permission for it included with the rest of the land we could always deal with it separately as an ALMO.'

Auriole Allen sat up smartly and said, 'I may have the body of a weak and feeble woman but I do have the heart and stomach of a public relations consultant. What in the name of goodness is an ALMO?'

'Arm's Length Management Operation,' explained Robert Selby.

'Modus Operandi,' put in Randolph Mansfield in a long-suffering voice.

Selby ignored him. 'And let me tell you, Auriole, an ALMO's nothing like as profitable as a hands-on one.'

'Easier to manage, though,' said Derek Hitchin comfortably.

'Less work for you, you mean,' said Selby uncharitably.

'Less hassle for everybody,' retorted Hitchin, 'except that in this case it won't wash. Our access road goes bang through the middle of it.'

'Now then, guys, ease up,' said Lionel Perry, very much the chairman. 'It's early days and nothing's settled yet.'

Before anyone could react to this, there was a tap on the door and a ginger-haired young man appeared, bearing a folder.

'Come in, er...' said the chairman, who had forgotten the employee's name. He deliberately avoided catching Auriole Allen's eye as he said it. He knew without being reminded that he wasn't any longer allowed to address the young women in the firm as 'my dear'; he wasn't even sure now whether 'my boy' had actionable overtones too. He decided against saying anything.

'Edward – well, Ned, actually,' said the young man helpfully, handing over the folder to the Finance Controller. 'Ned Phillips. I'm new here.'

'Ah, thank you, Ned,' said Robert Selby, taking the folder from the man and flipping it open. 'I'll need these figures presently.'

'You're settling in well, I hope,' said the chairman beaming benevolently at the newcomer. 'Liking it at Berebury Homes and all that?'

Ned Phillips said politely that he was finding life at Berebury Homes very interesting, thank you. He had a pleasant, unaffected voice and held himself well. He seemed notably unfazed by being in the presence of the firm's top brass.

'Good, good,' said Lionel Perry automatically.

'That's all, Ned, thanks,' began Robert Selby, looking over the documents and getting ready to resume his dire warnings.

'Just a minute, er – Ned, did you say?' The chairman began fumbling in his pocket and brought out a bunch of keys. 'You might just run my car down to Berebury Motors – that's the garage in the High Street, if you don't know it – and get them to mend the puncture in my spare wheel. I had a flat on the way in this morning.'

'No problem,' said Phillips, picking up the keys. 'It's the Jaguar in the chairman's parking bay, isn't it?'

Perry nodded. 'Tell them I need it done pronto. I've got another engagement quite soon after this.'

'If you ask me, Randolph,' said Derek Hitchin, deliberately provocative, as Ned Phillips withdrew, jangling the car keys in his hand, 'these old buildings are mostly white elephants.'

'Even white elephants have ivory tusks,' murmured Lionel Perry, almost to himself.

Hitchin gave another snort and turned back to Robert Selby. 'Now, a minute or two ago our financial controller was going to tell us something which began with "otherwise", remember? What was it, Robert? Tell us.'

'Otherwise,' replied Robert Selby flatly, 'if we don't get all the planning permissions we need, not only will we be unable to go ahead with any development at all but we'll be lumbered with repairing a grade two starred listed building to the local Council's standards and left in no condition to fight off Calleshire Construction's hostile approaches or those of anyone else who takes it into their head that we're ripe for development. That's right, Randolph, isn't it?'

Nobody, but nobody, called the architect "Randy".

'Not just repairing it,' Randolph Mansfield, the architect, came back in on the instant. 'Restoring it, which is very different. And worse. Much worse.'

'Then I'm afraid you'd be talking big money,' said Robert Selby. 'Really big.'

'There's just one other thing,' Lionel Perry picked up a piece of paper on the table in front of him, 'which I think I should bring to your attention. Someone called Stuart Bellamy...' he paused, looked round the table and asked, 'Does that name ring any bells with anyone?'

There was a concerted shaking of heads.

'Anyway, this Stuart Bellamy, whoever he is, wants to buy Tolmie Park and all the accompanying land.'

'Just like that?' said Derek Hitchin.

'Just like that,' said Lionel Perry richly. 'He says that if we would be kind enough to refer him to whoever it is who handles our legal matters, he will supply the appropriate references and so forth and then make us an offer.'

'He does, does he?' said Derek Hitchin.

Robert Selby, ever the finance man, frowned. 'He could be a straw man for Calleford Construction. I wouldn't put anything past them.'

This brought all the others up with a jerk. Calleford Construction Ltd had been jockeying for some time to be in a position from which to execute a takeover of Berebury Homes.

'That's a thought, Robert,' frowned Lionel Perry. 'Although I must say this approach doesn't look – well, big enough for that. It could just be some nutter trying to have us on.'

'Or it could be a bit of cloak and dagger stuff from Calleshire Construction,' persisted Selby.

Lionel Perry handed the letter over. 'Look into it anyway, will you, Robert, and find out what he's up to?' One eye on the clock, he gathered up his papers and closed the meeting. He forbore to remind them that on the other hand they were talking very big money indeed if Berebury Homes' development plans were to get the go-ahead without let or hindrance – with or without their rivals Calleford Construction muscling in.

Nobody could guess quite how big.

'Ah, there you are, Inspector,' the fire officer picked his way hurriedly over an intricate cobweb of hoses lying on the ground to greet the two policemen. 'Burton's the name, Charlie Burton.' He waved an arm in the direction of clouds of black smoke billowing up from behind the house, adding unnecessarily, 'And that's where our fire was.'

'At the back,' agreed Sloan, scanning the big old house, neglected but standing nevertheless. 'Still at the back, too,' he said.

Burton pushed his helmet back and grimaced. 'Contained so far. Not that you can ever be sure. Not with fire.'

'You never can tell with bees, either,' murmured Detective Constable Crosby at Sloan's elbow.

'Can't make any promises at all at this stage about when you'll be able to go in either,' said the fire officer. 'All I can say is that it hasn't spread into the really old part of the house.' He turned and pointed in the direction of a stand of trees beyond the side of the house. 'Luckily there's still plenty of water in the old lake over there otherwise I don't know what we'd have done out here in the back of nowhere.'

Detective Inspector Sloan followed his gaze over what had once been lawn and was now field in the direction of what had probably been designed as ornamental water.

'We haven't half upset the water lilies,' said Burton. 'But this is the way to go. Follow me.'

Sloan said, a little puzzled, 'I thought the place was supposed to be empty.'

'It was,' said the man drily. 'There was some printing business in here at one time but that took itself off when we got round to doing a fire check for their Safety at Work Certificate.'

'Not safe?' said Crosby.

'Electrical wiring out of the Ark,' said Charlie Burton. 'And the insulation was as rotten as it could get.'

'Perhaps that's what went wrong today,' suggested Detective Inspector Sloan.

'No, no, it's not an electrical fire,' said Burton, his professional expertise aroused. 'There's a bit more to it than that. If you ask me, ten to one it's arson. You'll see why in a tick. Our expert's on her way over as we speak but whatever you say, Inspector, nobody'll be able to do anything until the site's cooled down a bit.'

Detective Inspector Sloan nodded his understanding that there were would be forensic experts in the fire service, too.

'Nobody,' repeated Burton, tilting his helmet back.

'This fire...' began Detective Inspector Sloan, on duty and busy.

'We reckon we doused it before it got a hold on the main building,' said the fire officer. 'Easily. The billiard room was only added on, not integral.'

'Lucky you got here in time, though,' said Sloan.

Burton looked unhappy. 'I'm not so sure that we did.'

Sloan looked round the deserted garden and then at the remains of the parkland. 'You can't see anything of the place from the road so it was lucky that you got here at all.'

'Lucky, nothing,' said the fireman pithily. 'We had a call – an anonymous call from a public telephone kiosk.'

'You'll have it recorded, though,' murmured Sloan. All the services recorded everything these days: too much for the liking of some.

'Switchboard said it sounded as if it was spoken through a handkerchief or something,' said the fire officer.

'Disguised,' deduced Detective Constable Crosby from the sidelines.

'A man's voice, that's all they can say,' said the fireman.

Detective Inspector Sloan was not surprised. Most of the fire-setters he had encountered had been male – and young.

'We've traced it to a call box out on the road towards Almstone,' said Burton.

'Not the one in the village, then.' At the back of his mind Sloan had the thought that the other public telephone booth in Tolmie was next to the post office bang in the middle of the village High Street. Someone else must have known that too, then. He looked quizzically at the fire officer. 'If you know all that, why did you want us out here?'

'You'll see.' Charlie Burton's expression changed and he suddenly became very businesslike. 'Come this way, Inspector.' He led the way round the side of the house, picking his way round the snaking hoses once more. 'Just follow me, both of you, but mind how you go. We don't want any more accidents.'

'*More* accidents?' said Detective Constable Crosby, perking up.

'That's what I said.' He pursed his lips and said 'At least, I hope it was an accident.'

The two policemen followed the fire officer in single file, one behind the other, each following in the footsteps of the one ahead, none willing to step on any of the full hosepipes. As they got nearer to the back of the house they could hear the hissing of cold water on hot wood above the steady throb of the water pump.

There were firemen and a-plenty in action, tackling the site of the fire with practiced efficiency. The fire officer advanced to the side of the single-storey building least damaged by the flames.

'Come this way but mind how you go,' he said, indicating a window that had once held glass. 'You can see inside from here.'

Sloan clambered over a melange of wet wood, brick and glass to the fireman's side.

'Now take a look through there, Inspector,' Charlie Burton said, jerking his thumb. 'You may have to wait a moment for the smoke to clear enough for you to see what we saw.'

Detective Inspector Sloan approached the window space and peered into the building. There were no flames to be seen now but amid the swirling smoke he could make out exactly why it was the Criminal Investigation Department of the Force had been sent for by the fire brigade.

In the middle of the floor was a small pile of what were undoubtedly bones.

CHAPTER THREE

'Bones?' spluttered Superintendent Leeyes down the telephone. 'You're sure?'

'Bones,' said Detective Inspector Sloan. 'Definitely bones.'

'What sort of bones?' demanded Superintendent Leeyes peremptorily.

'I'm afraid I couldn't say, sir. I didn't get a very good look at them before the roof caved in.'

'Are you talking about a skeleton?' asked Leeyes from the comfort of his office back in Berebury.

'They might have come from one once,' replied Sloan, choosing his words with care, 'but what I saw looked like just a heap of bones.'

'*Disjecta membra*, then,' said Leeyes.

'Beg pardon, sir?' Sloan was perched uncomfortably among hoses snaking everywhere.

'Scattered limbs.' The superintendent was a regular member of Adult Education Classes. The one on 'Latin For All' had left its mark on the man. And on those at the police station, too.

'Dismembered ones, anyway,' ventured Sloan. 'We've determined it a crime scene for starters and Dr Dabbe's on his way over here now.' He'd left Crosby sealing off the site with what the constable persisted in calling tinsel tape.

The superintendent's grunt underlined his ingrained mistrust of professionals. Dr Hector Smithson Dabbe was the consultant pathologist for their part of the county of Calleshire and therefore not sufficiently in awe of senior policemen for the superintendent's liking.

'Not that he'll be able to see any more than we did at this stage.' Sloan paused to consider how to give his superior officer the unwelcome news that the fire brigade had already staked their claim to make their own investigation, Superintendent Leeyes being strong on the territorial imperative. 'The whole site's still very hot.'

'That won't stop him,' forecast Leeyes. 'Even if you won't give him the go-ahead.'

'No, sir. Probably not.' He could only agree with this. The good doctor had a reputation for getting the bit between the teeth.

'Go on, man.' The sound of the superintendent's fingers being drummed on a desk in Berebury was clearly audible down the telephone line. 'What next?'

'I am informed, sir, that the fire people have already initiated their own enquiries…' Sloan hurried on in response to a low growl down the telephone line, 'as they naturally have reason to believe that arson is involved, too.'

This was rewarded with another grunt. 'Do we have any incendiarists on record?'

'Not that I know of.'

'Or pyromaniacs?'

'I'm looking that up now,' said Sloan. 'I shall need to check on missing persons, too.'

'Missing for quite a while,' observed the superintendent acidly, 'if they were down to the bones.'

'Quite so,' said Sloan. 'But I think all we can do at this stage is to wait for everything to cool down.'

'Tolmie Park,' Superintendent Leeyes mused aloud. 'That rings a bell...'

'It's the painting of the house out here that I understand has gone missing after the break-in at the Greatorex Museum,' Sloan reminded him. 'Or, rather, a painting of one of the family with the house in the background.'

'Can't be a coincidence, that, Sloan,' growled the superintendent.

'No, sir.' No matter how much defence counsel could – and usually did – make of the benign statistics of coincidence the police were inclined to a more realistic view, circumstantial evidence being better than none.

'But there's something else about the place that I should remember, surely?'

'That's right, sir. It was Tolmie Park that the Calleshire and County Bank had all that trouble with two or three years ago. At least they called it trouble – we called it fraud.'

'If I remember rightly, Sloan, at the time I wanted to call it grand larceny.' He sniffed. 'But the bank wouldn't bring an action, would they?'

'Bad for business was what they said that would have been,' pointed out Sloan.

'Keeping mistakes in the family is what I call it,' said the superintendent vigorously. 'Not good.'

'Banks like doing that,' said Sloan.

'They caught a nasty cold, though, if their figures were

correct. And one, I may say, that they kept very quiet about.'

'Banks do. I expect they just called it a loan that went wrong,' said Sloan, 'and adjusted their books accordingly.' The finances of the Sloan *ménage* were straitened by a mortgage that was just – but only just – manageable.

'Call it whatever you like,' responded the superintendent briskly. 'Me, I still say it was larceny.'

'A money matter, anyway,' conceded Sloan.

'It wouldn't surprise me a hill of beans if this fire was, too,' prophesied the superintendent. 'Most trouble is.'

Somewhere where the news of the fire was received with shock mingled with disbelief was at the council offices in Berebury.

'Fire?' squeaked Melanie Smithers, the conservation officer there. She was young, plump and earnest. She was also dedicated to her job. 'Are you saying Tolmie Park is on fire?'

'Too true, I am,' said Jeremy Stratton coolly. He worked in the council's planning department. 'Someone's just rung in to tell us and accuse the developers of designer vandalism.'

'But,' she stammered, 'they didn't need to do that.'

'I'm not saying they did,' said the man from planning patiently. 'I'm just saying that someone else is saying so.'

'Who?'

'Anonymous call.'

'Vandals, I expect,' she said.

Jeremy Stratton leant negligently against the door post and drawled, 'Now who exactly are we talking about when we use the word vandals? Developers or the local yobbos? Personally, as far as the damage they do to the environment, I find it hard to tell the difference.'

'But,' wailed Melanie Smithers, 'they've only just put in for enabling planning permission. You must know that.'

'Oh, yes,' he said sardonically, 'we know that all right.'

Melanie Smithers reached for her hard hat. 'How big a fire?'

'They didn't say that either,' said the planning officer. The planning and conservation sections of the council were often at odds. This time he felt he had the edge. 'They might have put in for enabling development all right but they haven't got it yet, have they?'

'There were no delays in my section,' she retorted hotly. 'Tolmie Park is part of Calleshire's built heritage and we want it restored and kept safe.'

'It would seem that somebody doesn't,' he said pointedly.

'And granting permission for enabling development is the only way you can be sure these days,' said the girl. 'Unless you find a genuine benefactor prepared to do the restoration for love.'

'But you don't need enabling development if there's nothing to preserve, do you?' he grinned, starting to withdraw to his own office.

'There's that beautiful old house,' said Melanie Smithers as she struggled with difficulty into her high-visibility yellow jacket, 'just waiting for the right people to come along.'

'There's all that land, too,' said Jeremy Stratton.

'We at Conservation don't mind so much about that,' she said, grabbing her files and making for the door.

'Somebody does,' he said softly to her departing back. 'They mind very much.'

* * *

'I knew it! I knew it!' cried Wendy Pullman in anguish. She put down the telephone and turned to her husband. 'Oh, Paul, that was Jonathon Ayling.'

'What's that maniac gone and done now?' sighed Paul Pullman.

'No, you don't understand. Jonathon hasn't done anything. It's awful. He says he's just heard that the developers have done exactly what we said they would do and set Tolmie Park on fire.'

Wendy Pullman was the chairman of the Berebury Preservation Society. It had been founded on a rising tide of enthusiasm after the successful rescue of an endangered windmill in Larking village. Although even their best efforts had not been enough to save the last working forge in Calleshire over at Cullingoak – the giant leather bellows were now in the hands of a private collector – undeterred, they had proceeded to take up the cudgels in the cause of saving Tolmie Park from the developers with undiminished vigour. Their society's motto was 'Rebels With a Cause'.

'Is Jonathon sure it's them?' asked Paul Pullman reasonably.

His wife brushed this aside. 'Stands to reason, doesn't it? Nobody else has anything to gain.' She paused and then said 'He sounded quite – well, het-up. You know how excited Jonathon gets at the least little thing as far as preservation is concerned. But a fire…'

Paul Pullman, a preternaturally serious young man, nodded sagely. 'It was always on the cards that something like this would happen. We all knew that. The developers must have been looking for a quick way out of their planning troubles and taken it.'

'But they go and do it after all we've done to try to save that beautiful building,' said his wife tearfully. 'It's not fair.'

Wendy moved over to her desk in the corner of the room and searched for a file. The fact that their headquarters were situated in the Pullman's sitting room did not detract from the importance of the society in the eyes of its members. On the contrary, in fact, as it meant that one or other of the Pullmans was usually on the spot to deal with any sudden threats to existing old buildings.

'They're nothing but vandals,' she wailed.

'They're businessmen,' her husband reminded her. 'In it for the money.'

'Don't they have souls?' she asked rhetorically.

'They have shareholders,' said Paul Pullman.

'But what can we do now?' she asked. 'That's what Jonathon wants to know. That's why he rang.'

Paul Pullman stroked a non-existent beard and looked very wise. 'I'm not quite sure of the best course of action at this particular stage but I would say…'

He was interrupted in the delivery of his carefully considered opinion by the ringing of the telephone.

Wendy picked it up. 'Who? Ah, yes, of course.' She leant over and hissed in her husband's ear, 'It's a reporter from the *Berebury Gazette*.' She straightened up and said into the telephone 'Yes, I'm the chairman of the Berebury Preservation Society. Of course, I'm happy to make a statement for your publication.'

She motioned to Paul to hand her the file from the table and switched her voice into careful public relations mode. 'Tolmie Park is a very beautiful building, dating originally from about

1620. It was restyled in the early eighteenth century in the time of the fourth baronet,' although she had the file in her hands, she had the details off by heart, 'by the architect Colen Campbell – that's Colen with an "e". Got that? Good.'

She paused and rolled her eyes at Paul and then resumed her lecturing mode. 'Colen Campbell remodelled it in the harmonic mode much used by classical architects at the time, which is what makes it so important. What's that?'

There was another pause.

'Oh, I see what you mean,' said Wendy. 'Not a lot of it about any longer. Quite so.' Then she said in a very different tone of voice. 'Yes, of course, we know all about the house. That is why we are so keen to preserve it for future generations.'

Paul nodded approvingly at what she was saying. She grimaced at him in return but went on addressing the telephone as if she were on a platform.

'Further landscape work was done at the turn of the nineteenth century by the famous gardener Humphry Repton. That's Humphry without an *e*. Repton's got one, of course. Got what? An *e*, of course. In Repton.' She covered the mouthpiece and hissed at her husband. 'Don't these people know anything at all?'

She applied herself to the telephone again, listening rather more carefully when it became apparent that the newspaper reporter knew quite a lot.

'Oh, I see,' she said at last. 'Quite a small fire, confined to the old billiard room by the fire brigade. That's all right, then.' There was a pause. 'Why what? Why is it all right? Because the billiard room's only Victorian.' She stiffened and said coldly down the telephone. 'Of course our society is interested in the preservation of Victorian buildings, too, it's just that Tolmie Park is basically an older building.'

There was another pause while Wendy listened rather more attentively.

'Yes,' she said eventually. 'We know all about the planning application to build all those houses in the grounds – yes, that's right – they call it enabling development. That's so they can spend the money they make on those houses on restoring the house. In theory,' she added richly.

It became evident that the newspaper reporter had not needed having this spelt out for him.

'Our concern,' said Wendy loftily, overlooking this, 'is that Tolmie Park becomes a jewel in Calleshire's crown once again.'

The telephone crackled.

'No,' she said firmly, 'not even with enabling development. Nobody wants dozens of nasty little houses all over the park spoiling the whole ambience.'

Paul Pullman looked distinctly uneasy as she replaced the telephone. 'I'm not sure you should have said that, Wendy.'

'I shall deny that I did,' she said serenely. She blew him a kiss. 'And say I was misquoted. Or taken out of context. That's what they always say, isn't it? You didn't hear it anyway, did you, darling?' She picked up the telephone again. 'I'd better ring Jonathon back and make sure he doesn't do anything silly this time.'

CHAPTER FOUR

Detective Inspector Sloan stepped gingerly over the fire hoses, trying in vain to avoid the puddles of water in between. He heard Dr Dabbe and his perennially taciturn assistant, Burns, arrive at Tolmie Park long before he saw the consultant pathologist's car come round the corner of the building at a smart pace and screech to a halt.

'Ah, there you are, Sloan,' said the doctor, climbing out of his vehicle and slamming the car door behind him. 'Now, what have you got for us this time?'

'Not a lot, I'm afraid,' said the policeman.

'Size is immaterial in pathology,' said Dabbe jovially. 'That right, Burns?'

'Yes, doctor,' said his assistant, before setting about unpacking some rubber boots from the cases he had brought along.

'You'd be surprised at how small some of the evidence I deal with is,' said the pathologist chattily. 'Take microbes, for instance...can't get much smaller than them and they kill quicker than most.'

'All we've got to go on here,' said Sloan, sticking to the matter in hand, 'is what we – that is, the fire people and ourselves – saw before the roof went.'

'And that was?' asked the doctor, starting to struggle into white overalls.

'Bones,' said Sloan. 'They were in a small heap in the middle of the floor.'

'Now you see them, now you don't,' murmured Detective Constable Crosby to no one in particular.

'The fire,' hurried on Sloan, 'has been confined to a later addition to the house – a billiard room at the back.'

'The Victorians slapped them on,' said the pathologist, 'for their angry young men.'

'Come again,' said Detective Constable Crosby, perking up. 'Nobody ever put up a building for me.'

'Billiard rooms,' said the pathologist succinctly, 'were an early form of birth control.'

'Pull the other one,' murmured Crosby almost under his breath.

Dr Dabbe said solemnly 'It's true. They used to put their sons in there with a billiard table and no women. Kept their hands busy.'

'But...' began Crosby.

'And,' swept on the doctor, 'since quite a lot of them were called Septimus and Octavious you can see their problem.'

'Our problem...' started Sloan.

'Is a burnt offering now, I should say from the looks of things,' said Dabbe, taking in the charred beams and a building open to the sky in one swift glance.

'Now, perhaps,' pointed out Sloan. 'The bones didn't look all that burnt when I saw them.'

'Not a lot to go on, then, Sloan,' said the pathologist. 'A memory of bones.'

'No, doctor.'

Dabbe stroked his chin. 'I don't think we've ever had as little as that for starters, have we, Burns? Just a memory.'

His assistant shook his head and said lugubriously. 'Not so far, doctor.'

'And was, as the Old Testament puts it so well, Sloan, the knee bone connected to the thigh bone, so to speak?'

'Not that I saw,' said Sloan a little stiffly, 'but as I said, doctor, I didn't get a really good look.'

'Dem bones…' began Crosby until quelled into silence by a look from Sloan. 'Sorry, sir.'

'All I know is that the fire officer over there,' Sloan waved in the direction of Charlie Burton, 'is talking of a suspicious cause for what he calls this minor conflagration.' Every calling had its own argot and the Fire and Rescue Service was no different from all the others. Doctors and lawyers were worse. They spoke in theirs all the time.

'What sort of bones?' asked Dr Dabbe. 'We're not talking of a tramp's supper gone wrong, are we?'

'I don't know, doctor,' said Sloan. 'All we saw was this heap in the middle of the room. The fire chap with a camcorder – they video everything these days, you know – tried to get a decent picture but the roof fell in while he was doing it.'

Dr Dabbe stared up at the charred rafters of the billiard room. 'Didn't this place have a bit of a reputation at one time?'

'A long time ago,' said Detective Inspector Sloan. If it had one now he, as head of the tiny Criminal Investigation Department at F Division at Berebury, would have heard of it, even if it had not yet come to the official attention of the police. For starters, the local bobby would have been sure to have mentioned the fact in one of his reports. And rumour, that swift, if not sure, traveller, would have brought news of any strange goings-on to his attention very soon. 'Once. In history,' he added for good measure. 'Not now.'

'In the field of forensic pathology, Sloan, we only ever deal in things that have already happened,' said Dr Dabbe amiably. 'That right, Burns?'

'Yes, doctor,' responded the man dutifully. 'Your thermometer…'

'In our line of country we leave the present and the future to others,' said the pathologist, nevertheless peering acutely at the smouldering detritus on the floor of the billiard room and advancing to record the ambient temperature.

'Your rubber gloves, doctor,' said Burns, delving into his bags and coming up with a succession of items for all the world as if it were a lucky dip.

'I don't know that I'm going to need them,' said Dabbe. 'Not until everything cools down a bit.' He cast his eyes round the site again and then pointed towards Charlie Burton. 'Have the fire people got any ideas on where the seat of the fire was?'

'It's a bit strange, that.' Sloan frowned. 'Their first thoughts – they won't say for certain, naturally – is that it was started…'

'Was started?'

'They think they've found evidence of an accelerant…' said Sloan.

'I never did believe in spontaneous combustion,' said Dr Dabbe.

'…In one of the corners furthest away from the main building.'

'Not under the bones, then.'

'It would seem not.'

'If the intention was to incinerate them,' mused the pathologist, 'then they didn't go the right way about it.'

'Our thinking, too,' said Sloan magnanimously, since as far as he could tell, Crosby hadn't had any thoughts at all. It was a point to be noted, though.

'But if the intention was that the bones were to be seen at some point...'

'Ah,' said Sloan.

'Then starting the fire at a distance...'

'And alerting the fire brigade,' put in Sloan.

'Then you achieve your object,' observed the pathologist astutely. 'Interesting, that, Sloan.'

'And so is the fact that the fire didn't get to the main building before the fire engines got here,' said Detective Inspector Sloan, making another note.

'That you, Stu?' called out Jason Burke throatily as Bellamy came through the door.

'It is. What's up?' said Stuart Bellamy. He knew the sound of Burke's voice well enough by now to recognise when a certain tone meant trouble.

'What have you been and gone done now, Stu?' asked Burke silkily.

'Me? I haven't done anything, Jason. Why?'

'Someone has. And if it isn't you then I don't know who it is.' Burke seized a nearby guitar and began to play a tune on it.

'Who has done what?' demanded Stuart in matching forthright tones.

'I said buy it, man, not burn it down.' The strumming increased in volume.

'I still don't get it, Jas,' said Bellamy, hanging his jacket over the back of a chair. 'Burn what down?'

'Tolmie Park.'

'Strewth. You mean they've…?'

'Set Tolmie Park on fire. They've just said so on the local news.' Jason Burke belonged to a generation that couldn't manage without background noise. He kept the radio on all the time. He didn't diminish the volume of his guitar-playing.

'Well, it wasn't me, I can promise you, mate.'

'You're sure you haven't gone and done it so you don't have the hassle of buying the place?'

'Quite sure,' said Bellamy, as ever surprised by his employer's limited horizons. 'All I did was write and tell the head honcho at Berebury Homes that we wanted to buy the estate, like you said.'

'So why would they try to burn it down just when I wanted to buy it?' Burke, always inclined to the personal, sounded puzzled rather than cross.

'Search me, Jason. I just asked them to tell me who we could talk turkey with. That's all. I promise you.'

'What did they say?' Burke appeared now to be giving all his attention to an iPod but Stuart Bellamy knew him too well to be taken in by this.

'They said they weren't selling,' said Bellamy. 'Not no way. Their boss man – he's called Lionel Perry – rang me up. He got quite upset at the idea of parting with the place.'

'You didn't tell them it was me, did you?' Jason Burke, who had an excellent instinct for personal publicity, also knew very well the importance of keeping a low profile when he wanted to buy anything. This, the young star was well aware, was a time that called for keeping the well-known head well below the parapet.

''Course not,' said Bellamy. 'That would have pushed the price up like anything. We both know that. No, I only used my own name and that wouldn't have meant a thing to anyone.' There were some occasions when he was very glad about that and this was one of them.

'I know there are people who don't enjoy our sort of concert,' went on the pop musician earnestly, still puzzled, 'but blow me, not enough to want to burn a place to the ground so I can't buy it, surely.'

'Sure, Jas.' Stuart Bellamy saw no point in trying to explain to the pop star that not everyone liked the decibel levels reached by the famous Kevin Cowlick events and that the Summer of Love hadn't gone down too well with the older generation.

'That's just what makes Tolmie Park the perfect spot for concerts,' explained the pop musician. 'The isolation. Not having anyone living near enough to have a reason to complain will be a great help.'

'I can see that,' said Stuart Bellamy, accountant marque. For a boy from the back streets of the industrial town of Luston, Jason Burke also had a very good grasp of what constituted a viable business proposition. 'No one would have heard a thing from Tolmie Park, it's so far out in the country.'

'A bit less of that "would have", Stu, if you don't mind,' said Jason, demonstrating that he had a better feeling for the

English language than might have been thought by most of his audiences, especially after a vocal event, 'because I still want it. Ruin or not. And not just because it's a good place for a rave…' he grinned and looked suddenly quite sheepish. 'Sorry, I've got to say "festival", haven't I? Not rave.'

'You have if you want to get it past the council's committees,' said Bellamy feelingly. 'They're mostly of an age to have Woodstock engraved on their hearts, remember.'

'Right. Festival, it is. But I still want Tolmie Park. That understood?' There was no mistaking the undertone of menace in his voice now.

'Perfectly.'

'And Stu…'

'Yes?'

'Go find out who started that fire.'

'Will do.'

'And pronto.'

'Sure thing. And I'll try to find out as well why they did, Jason. That matters, too, don't forget.' Stuart Bellamy pulled out his chair and sat down. As he did so he reminded himself of that aphorism that the familiar is not necessarily the known. If anything described his relationship with Jason Burke, that was it.

How Melanie Smithers, Berebury Council's conservation officer, got through the cordon of tape Crosby had put up round the burnt shell of the billiard room, Detective Inspector Sloan never knew. The first he saw of that young woman was when her well-covered figure appeared at his elbow, hard-hat, steel-capped boots and all.

'I'm afraid, miss, that whoever you are, I must ask you to leave,' he said, putting up an arm to stop her advancing any further towards the smouldering building. 'At once.'

'Please, I just want to see...'

'I must warn you, miss,' Sloan interrupted her sternly, 'that if you don't go straight back to the main road, you could be at risk of prosecution for interfering with the police in the execution of their duties.'

'And the police could be accused of interfering with me in performing mine,' she countered unexpectedly, 'if you don't let me stay.'

'And what might they be?' he enquired, interested in spite of himself.

'Making sure that the fire brigade doesn't do any more damage than they need to,' she came back swiftly. 'Or the developers. Give either of them half a chance and they'll be getting a structural engineer round to say that they should be knocking down what's left of this end of the house on safety grounds even though it's a listed building before I've had a chance to take photographs and do some measurements. I know what they're like. Both of them.'

'All the while this is a crime scene nobody's touching anything until I say so,' pronounced Detective Inspector Sloan, his authority grounded in statute law. 'That goes for you, miss, and the fire brigade and everybody else.'

It didn't, unfortunately, seem to have gone for Dr Dabbe. The pathologist was now lying flat on the ground on his tummy, a pair of binoculars glued to his eyes. They were pointing in the direction of a pile of charred rafters heaped on what had been the parquet floor of the billiard room. 'I just need to get them properly focused,' he said to nobody in particular, 'and I might see something.'

'That's all I want to do, too,' pleaded Melanie Smithers, still at Sloan's elbow. 'See something.'

'Back to the main road,' repeated Sloan. 'Now.'

'Please, Inspector – it is Inspector, isn't it? – all I need is a really good look at exactly where this new building joins on to the old one before anyone starts knocking it about.'

'What new building?' asked Sloan.

'The Victorian one.' She dismissed the wrecked billiard room with a wave of her hand. 'It's very important that I take a look now.'

'And why won't it wait?' asked Sloan with professional curiosity. The good books on policing stressed that note should always be taken of all those at the scene of any incident, but especially those very near and anxious to speak there and then. 'Everything's going to be much too hot to touch for hours.'

'Because the developers will want as much of the building pulled down as soon as they can,' she said. 'I'm the local conservation officer and I know just how they operate.'

'Fast?' suggested Crosby, drawn to Sloan's side and his interest engaged by the presence of a pretty young girl.

'They'll get some demolition people in with the speed of light if they possibly can,' she said, 'and get the work all carried out with the speed of light under any pretext they can dream up.'

'It's a white elephant, then, is it?' said Crosby, waving an arm in the direction of the house.

Melanie Smithers made a face. 'If you ask me, as far as the

developers are concerned the whole of Tolmie Park here isn't so much a white elephant as an albatross round their necks.'

Detective Inspector Sloan's mind had been working along quite different lines and the *Rime of the Ancient Mariner* hadn't come into it. He said casually, 'Could the house that you're talking about by any chance have been the one shown on the painting of Tolmie Park in the museum?'

She turned an eager face to him. 'That's right, Inspector. How did you know that? In the Filligree portrait there. But this later part...'

'Later?' he said.

'Well, Victorian, anyway...' she nodded quickly. 'We think that at the point where it was joined on to the old building that you ought now to be able to see the obscured parts of an even older building. The original core, so to speak.'

'The nearly new, the old and the very old,' remarked Crosby.

'The very oldest parts were probably the remnants of a cross wing,' said Melanie Smithers, taking this seriously. 'With a bit of luck they were still visible as part of the existing Tolmie Park when the painting was done.' She sniffed. 'Most of the remains were probably cleared away when they put up the billiard room. They were so ignorant in those days.'

'I see,' said Sloan. He didn't see anything except that it was important to her. And therefore perhaps to the police. That is, if the portrait missing from the museum with its old view of the house had anything to do with the fire and the bones. Melanie Smithers didn't know about the bones. At least, he hoped she didn't.

'What sort of old building would it have been you were looking for, miss?' he asked.

'Early medieval.'

'Early Filligrees?'

'No, no. Not the Filligrees,' she said dismissively. 'They were only sixteenth-century parvenus.' She looked at the two policemen. 'You know, Johnnies-come-lately.'

'Up like a rocket, down like stone,' intoned Crosby.

'A lot of people made money then,' she said seriously. 'Mostly under Henry the Eighth.'

Detective Constable Crosby started to hum the ditty, "I'm 'Enery the Eighth, I am, I am",' under his breath.

'And Queen Elizabeth,' said the young woman. 'The Filligrees tried to curry favour with her by raising a regiment here at Tolmie.'

'Good Queen Bess,' said Crosby.

'The document's still in the archive. *"For the Lords of the Privy Council having sent to Francis Filligree as well as others to get the militia in a readiness, he made a muster at Tolmie"* in 1599.' She scowled. 'The Muster Green is one of the places the developers want to build on.'

'So…' began Sloan.

'It was the Tolhursts who were the really old family here,' she said, 'but you know very few families last longer than three ash trees.'

'Three ash trees?' said Detective Constable Crosby, while Sloan added an ash tree to a mental list of bizarre English measurements that started with the length of Henry the Second's foot and thumb.

Melanie Smithers smiled sweetly at the detective constable

and explained that ash trees seldom lived longer than a hundred years.

Crosby's face cleared, while the conservation officer turned back, looked up at Sloan and said earnestly, 'So you see, Inspector, how important it is that we find out for sure about the first building, don't you?'

'But you're just guessing about there being bits of an old building here, aren't you?' said Sloan, deliberately provocative. They had a very different benchmark of importance down at the police station and that didn't include the early medieval.

Or the jumped-up.

No, that wasn't true. The jumped-up caused problems all of their own.

Melanie Smithers rose to her full height. 'I'm certainly not guessing. There's an old document in the Calleshire archives that's been dated to about 1430 which refers to *"Tymbr for ye Roffs at Tulmie"* and that's ages before this Tolmie Park was built – and then in 1441 Sir Lambert Tolhurst received a licence from King Henry VI to enclose, crenellate and furnish with towers and battlements his manor at Tolmie.'

'Was that to pour the boiling oil out of?' enquired Crosby with interest.

'Probably.' Melanie Smithers grinned. 'You had to get your permissions even then. It didn't all begin with the 1947 Town and Country Planning Act, you know.'

'And why is it so imperative that you find traces of this old building?' Sloan asked, undiverted. 'Isn't Tolmie Park old enough for you?'

'Sixteen hundred and something isn't as old as fourteen hundred,' she said ineluctably.

'Granted, miss,' said Sloan, 'but it doesn't answer my question.'

'If there was a really ancient site here,' she said, 'it would need excavating before there was any further development and that would help in our battle to keep the developers up to scratch as well as insisting that there is a full archaeological survey carried out before work gets started.'

'I see.' Wheels within wheels was what Sloan would have called that.

'They won't like it, of course,' she said.

'I can see that they mightn't,' said Sloan moderately, making another note.

'Besides…' her voice trailed away and she suddenly looked younger still.

'Besides…?' prompted Detective Inspector Sloan, a man experienced in picking out useful leads arising during the questioning of suspects – and a great practitioner of what was known as repetitive listening. It was surprising what an echo brought out: often enough more than a question did.

'Besides,' she grinned suddenly, 'I'm doing a master's degree in the medieval houses of Calleshire and being the first to record this one would be a real feather in my cap.'

CHAPTER FIVE

The second meeting to be held in the offices of Berebury
Homes Ltd that day was more focused but not so well-
structured as the first one had been. For one thing, the
meeting hadn't actually been called by anyone but had just
grown rather like Topsy as news of the fire at Tolmie Park
had spread through their building.

'Fire?' snapped Derek Hitchin, their project manager.
'You're quite sure, are you, Auriole?'

'The *Berebury Gazette* have just rung me for a quote on it,'
said Auriole Allen, adding ironically, 'I don't know how sure
that makes it but I told them that it was certainly news to all
of us here at Berebury Homes and they could certainly quote
me on that.'

'Let's hope it was,' said Robert Selby, the finance man,
sourly. 'There'll be hell to pay if not.'

'Where's Lionel?' asked Randolph Mansfield.

'On the golf course,' chorused Derek Hitchin and Robert
Selby in unison. 'Need you ask?'

'Should we tell him, I wonder?' mused Auriole Allen
thoughtfully. 'It might be better if he didn't know just yet.
Until he's been properly briefed and we've dealt with the
press, I mean.'

'Rather you than me,' said Hitchin, in whom the instinct for self-preservation was strong. 'He won't want anyone to think we've done it.'

'As we haven't, I don't think we need worry about that,' said Randolph Mansfield. He looked round at the others. 'Well, we haven't, have we?'

'No, of course not,' said Auriole Allen soothingly. She immediately undid the effect of this anodyne statement by going on, 'but we're bound to be suspected. You must see that.'

'Being the only outfit with anything to gain from a fire there,' said Robert Selby flatly. He always insisted that realism was part of his stock-in-trade and in any case also always insisted he was a man who thought solely in terms of gains and losses and that was what he was there for.

'Are you quite sure about that, Robert?' Hitchin said, studying the tips of his fingertips with unusual intensity. 'What about Calleshire Construction? They might find a hostile take-over a lot easier if we'd been wrong-footed somehow at Tolmie by the Conservation people.'

'Hit us when we were down, you mean?' said Randolph Mansfield.

'It's less trouble then,' said Robert Selby, adding sourly, 'you learnt that at school, remember?'

'Surely not, Derek,' protested Auriole Allen. 'You don't think that…?'

'I don't think at all,' said Derek Hitchin, 'but their boss-man isn't known as Tiger for nothing.'

'And we don't know for sure,' pointed out Mansfield, staring at the ceiling with apparent concentration, 'that it is actually a hostile bid that they've made. We only know about

Calleford Construction's bid exactly what Lionel chooses to tell us and nothing whatsoever more.'

A little silence fell on the group. Then Robert Selby said 'I think I'll just get young Ned to run over to the clubhouse and leave a note on Lionel's locker there. Then he won't be taken by surprise.'

There was another short silence broken this time by Hitchin saying slowly, 'Good idea.'

Having thus minded their backs so to speak, the four of them settled down to explore the new vistas opened up by the news.

'How much damage?' asked Randolph Mansfield.

'Confined to one part of the building, they say,' said Auriole Allen. 'The newspaper has got one of their photographers on his way there now.'

'Which part?' asked the architect urgently.

'The back.'

'That's good.' Randolph Mansfield heaved himself to his feet. 'Well, I suppose I'd better be getting over there myself to see what's what.'

'I'll come with you,' said Derek Hitchin, although normally he avoided the other man's company. 'A fire might affect things – open up possibilities and all that. You never know.'

'Just a minute, just a minute,' said Robert Selby. 'If we didn't do it and we suppose that Calleshire Construction didn't do it, then who did? This guy Bellamy?'

'My money's on that daft bananas outfit,' said Derek Hitchin.

'I don't know anything about a bananas outfit,' protested Auriole Allen.

'Yes, you do,' insisted the project manager. 'They call themselves the Berebury Preservation Society.'

'I still don't get it, Derek,' said the public relations woman. 'What've they got to do with bananas? Or are you saying they're just plain barmy?'

He spelt it out for her. '"Build Absolutely Nothing Anywhere Near Anyone". Bananas. Got it now, Auriole?'

Her face cleared and she nodded. 'I see.'

'And their Jonathon Ayling's quite up to a diversionary tactic like this,' said the project manager.

'Remember how he tried to save that old forge in Cullingoak?' said Selby. 'By getting a pal of his in the rubber trade to make the biggest balloon in the world. Then they fixed it to the end of the bellows.'

'And when they'd done that,' contributed Mansfield, 'they blew it up to show their message writ large.'

'Something rude?' hazarded Auriole.

'Very,' said Mansfield shortly.

'I'll say,' muttered Hitchin. 'About the conservation officer who wouldn't put a preservation order on it and the planning officer who let them build flats where the old forge had been.'

'Melanie Smithers and your old friend Jeremy Stratton?' hazarded Selby.

'How did you guess?' drawled Hitchin, unabashed.

The senior staff of Berebury Homes Ltd were not the only people considering the possible activities of Jonathon Ayling in connection with the mysterious fire at Tolmie Park. The members of the Berebury Preservation Society, too, were making quite sure that their backs were covered.

'Not me, guv,' said that young man to the hastily assembled committee of the Society, giving them his usual charming smile. 'Honest.'

'I must say that setting the building alight didn't seem the action of a dedicated preservationist,' said Paul Pullman austerely. In spite of being married to Wendy he still valued logical analysis of all situations.

'Whatever anyone says,' pronounced someone else with apparent irrelevance, 'there are always wheels within wheels.'

Jonathon Ayling said in his customary engaging manner, 'In the vernacular all I can say is "I never".'

'Then who did?' demanded Wendy Pullman.

'Ah, now you're asking,' he said turning his frank gaze on her. 'And that I can't tell you because I don't know.'

'Honest, Jonathon?' Had she but known it, Wendy would have made a good nursery school teacher. 'You're not leading us on, are you?'

'Cross my heart, Wendy, and hope to die. All I know is that it wasn't me.'

Paul Pullman asked sternly 'Or anyone you know?'

Jonathon Ayling shook his head. 'My mates are always willing to help the cause, naturally, but I don't think they'd have set a place on fire without being asked.'

'That means,' concluded Paul Pullman ineluctably, 'that they would have done it if you had.'

'Sure,' the young man said easily. 'That's what friends are for, isn't it?'

'Well, then, Jonathon,' temporised Wendy, 'we'll just have to take your word for it, won't we?'

He gave her the sweetest of smiles. 'That's right, Wendy.'

He looked round at the assembled company and said, 'That's if you all still want me on board.'

'Of course we do,' said someone at the back. 'We'd never have saved the Larking windmill without you.'

'And without our back-up campaign, too,' put in Wendy a little indignantly. 'Don't forget that. We wrote all the letters, remember…'

'But it was Jonathon perching on the cap on the top of the windmill that got the television people interested,' persisted the woman at the back.

'I don't think we should be fighting old battles…' began Paul Pullman, who thought of himself as the voice of reason.

'Did the trick, though, didn't it?' grinned Jonathon.

'Is this fire going to save Tolmie Park though?' asked Wendy Pullman in an attempt to resume the initiative.

'Only if we can utilise the delay to our advantage,' said another committee member.

'And step up our campaign,' seconded the woman at the back.

'Unless Jonathon has something up his sleeve?' suggested someone else hopefully.

'Something legal,' put in Paul Pullman.

Jonathon Ayling contrived to look injured. 'I haven't been caught doing anything that isn't straight-up yet, have I?'

'I wouldn't know,' said Paul Pullman, 'would I?'

His wife quite spoilt the effect of this by saying, 'And we don't want to know, either.'

'I don't think,' said the woman at the back seriously, 'that Jonathon should take that as our giving him carte blanche to act in whatever manner he thinks fit.'

'Of course not,' said Wendy instantly. 'We will always act within the law.'

'What would be a help,' said her husband acidly, 'is if everyone else did.' He turned to the young man at his side. 'And that goes for you, too, Jonathon, remember.'

Detective Constable Crosby was bored. Standing on sentry duty to one side of all the action was not his idea of fun – or policing. He therefore looked up with interest at the approach of a fresh face, and a fairly young one at that.

'Sorry, sir,' he said to the new arrival. 'No admittance beyond this point.'

'That's OK,' said Stuart Bellamy. 'I just came to see what's going on here.'

'A lot of fire-raisers do that,' remarked Crosby in an off-hand way. 'They like to see the fire engines and the flames. Touches the spot or something.'

'I know arsonists are usually male,' said Stuart Bellamy. 'It's not women's work and all that.'

'So what brings you?' asked Crosby, taking out his notebook. He wasn't hopeful of gleaning much useful information since the man had left his car in clear view but from force of habit he wrote down the registration number of the vehicle.

'Curiosity,' replied Stuart Bellamy immediately. 'You see, I'd just made an offer to buy the place…'

'Rather you than me,' said Crosby. 'I mean, just look at it – it's practically falling down as it is.'

'And it's beginning to look as if someone doesn't want me to have it,' said Stuart Bellamy, continuing his own train of thought.

'Does a bit, doesn't it?' agreed Crosby, looking over his shoulder at the smouldering building, and making a mental note to tell his superior officer just that. 'You can see that even without the fire that it's going to cost a pretty penny to put it right.'

The cost of repairing Tolmie Park was something Stuart Bellamy hadn't raised so far with Jason Burke. He knew what his answer would be if he did because it happened every time his manager warned the musician about spending big money. Jason would first quote his old granny, who had always said that it was your economies that you regretted, and then he would sing a couple of lines of an old song beginning, "There's a hole in your bucket, dear Liza, dear Liza."

This would evoke the peerless follow-on by Jason himself in a different key of "Then mend it, dear Liza, mend it, dear Liza," and a little lecture about if you had the money then there was no point in not spending it, was there? Even if Bellamy had finished his articles with the accountancy firm, he felt he would have had no answer to this.

Stuart Bellamy said aloud to Crosby now, 'And I wondered if you people had any idea of who might not want me to buy it?'

'Not at this stage, sir,' said Crosby magisterially. 'And, of course, if we had, I wouldn't be in a position to tell you. Now, if you would tell me your name and address I'll pass it on to the inspector in charge and keep you informed.'

In another part of the forest of charred timbers that had once comprised the roof of the billiard room at Tolmie Park, someone else besides the conservation officer was trying to wheedle his way past authority.

'No, doctor.'

'Just a few yards,' pleaded Dr Dabbe. He had risen to his feet, dusted off the trouser legs of his white suit and made for a point even further into the ruined room than before. 'I only want a *coup d'oeil*.'

'No, doctor,' repeated Charlie Burton, the fire officer. 'Whatever one of those may be, you can't have it.'

Undeterred, Dr Dabbe said 'I think if I went in only a little further up here, I might just get a slightly better look…'

'No, doctor.' The fire officer shook his head. 'Everything's still much too hot.'

'You see,' went on the pathologist persuasively, 'there is something very interesting about the little bit of bone that I can see from here.'

'That's as may be,' pronounced Charlie Burton authoritatively, 'but since there's no question of human life being at stake, it would be as much as my job's worth to let you get yourself burnt.'

'If what I'm looking at is the distal end of a femur,' continued Dr Dabbe as if the man had not spoken, 'then it's got a very funny medial condyle.'

'I don't care if it's got a serious one,' exploded the exasperated fire officer, 'you aren't going any further in until I say so.'

'And if I could just get a proper look at the trochantic fossa at the proximal end of that bone…' The pathologist started to inch his way forward again, binoculars at the ready, with all the enthusiasm of the specialist. 'I haven't had a case of excarnation for years.'

'And what's that when it's at home?' demanded the fireman in exasperation.

'Leaving bones out to be picked over. By the way, for the record I should say that the bones are sitting on some sort of calcined material. I can't quite see what.'

Charlie Burton clambered over some wreckage to get back to the side of Detective Inspector Sloan, hissing in his ear 'What part of "no" is it that he doesn't understand?'

Sloan regarded the prone figure of the pathologist advancing on his tummy with a certain dispassion. 'I would say that what the good doctor is looking for is wriggle room.'

'Very funny,' snapped Burton. 'Well, if you ask me I think he's going to get his fingers burnt.'

'His, though,' pointed out Sloan. 'Not ours.' Self-preservation was something learnt early on the beat.

'You stop him then, mate,' said the fireman, shrugging his shoulders. 'It's no skin off my nose if he does himself an injury.' Having thus metaphorically washed his hands of the matter, Charlie Burton started to move away. Then he stopped and said over his shoulder, 'But by my reckoning, nobody's supposed to enter a crime scene without your permission anyway.'

'And yours,' said Sloan politely.

'Mine?'

'Arson, I think you said.' Sloan waved a hand. 'The probable cause of the fire. It's a crime.'

'What? Oh, yes.' The man halted in his tracks and gave him a tight little smile. 'We leave all that to our investigative experts and they do like a clear field.'

Taking the hint, Detective Inspector Sloan advanced

towards the pathologist himself. 'Doctor, I must remind you that this is an active crime scene...'

'Not as far as I'm concerned, it isn't, Sloan, arson apart.'

'If those are human bones...'

'Ah, that's just it, Sloan,' said Dr Dabbe. 'I don't think they are.'

CHAPTER SIX

'Not human bones?' echoed Superintendent Leeyes indignantly. 'Is he sure?'

'That's what he says,' said Sloan. 'He can't really get close enough to them to be quite sure because of the heat so we haven't got his official report yet.'

'If they're not human bones, then what are they?' demanded Leeyes down the telephone line.

'His unconfirmed opinion is that they're animal but he can't get near enough to confirm that either until the whole place has cooled down. All he will say is that they are big and not human.'

'From our point of view I would have thought there were only two sorts of bones,' observed Leeyes loftily. 'Homo sapiens and the rest.'

'Quite so.' From a police perspective and animal cruelty apart, Sloan agreed with him. He said 'I'm afraid there could be a joker in the pack.'

Leeyes sniffed. 'Literally.'

Sloan forged on. 'I think it would be as well, sir, also to allow for the possibility that they could be either animal bones or artificial ones.'

'Like I said, someone having us on, do you think?' growled the superintendent.

Sloan coughed. 'Don't you remember, sir, that the Berebury Preservation Society has a bit of a reputation for the exotic? Their Jonathon Ayling's a bit of a wild card. What you might call their stunt-man.'

'Is it them who's doing it?' snorted Leeyes combatively. 'If so, then just wait until I...'

'We don't know yet that it's anyone,' said Sloan, adding sedulously, 'And, of course, sir, it may not be us that they're having on.'

'Who else then?' growled Leeyes, who was inclined to take things personally.

'There's the planning people for starters and then there's the developers.'

The superintendent wasn't listening. 'Sloan, you don't think that the bones could have come from an aurochs?' He sounded almost wistful.

'Sir?'

'The extinct European bison.'

'I couldn't say, I'm sure,' responded Sloan warily. The superintendent's expertise in some fields was as reliable as his lack of knowledge in others. The trouble was that members of the Force couldn't be certain of either.

'Also known as the urus or wild ox.'

'Really, sir?' That must have come from "Archaeology and Anthropology for the Uninitiated", an early evening class from which the superintendent had retired, hurt. This was after crossing swords with the lecturer on the thorny question of the descent of man – or, more specifically, the ancestry of criminal man.

'They had a collection of bones from one of them in the

museum. We went to see it.' Leeyes added, hit by a sudden thought, 'You don't suppose somebody's stolen them from the Paleolithic Room there, do you?'

'I'll check, sir,' promised Detective Inspector Sloan, adding that to his growing to-do list. 'The museum people didn't mention it this morning but there is definitely something very odd about the break-in there.'

'And don't try to tell me, Sloan,' said Leeyes, tacitly agreeing with this, 'that the nicking of that painting of Tolmie Park hours before the place was set on fire is just a coincidence.'

'I shan't,' promised Detective Inspector Sloan truthfully.

'Looking for Lionel Perry, are you?' said Jock Stirling, the professional at the Berebury golf club, to the ginger-haired young man standing in front of the counter in his shop.

Ned Phillips nodded.

Stirling jerked his shoulder towards the course. 'That's him and his pals just putting out at the seventeenth now.'

Phillips looked enquiringly in the direction of the course.

'Far right, middle distance,' said Stirling. 'As you can see, he's playing in a four-ball and they're always slow.'

'Is he any good?' asked Ned Phillips. 'At the game, I mean,' he added hastily.

'Not bad for his age,' responded Jock Stirling, reaching for a metal wood club and starting to polish the head with a soft duster. 'Not bad at all.'

Ned Phillips, who didn't realise that this was the other man's stock response to any enquiry about a member's play, nodded and said 'I've got a message for him from work.'

Jock Stirling sucked his lips. 'Me, I wouldn't want to disturb anyone's game. Not at the seventeenth. Not for anything less than an earthquake.'

'It wasn't an earthquake,' murmured Ned Phillips.

'Players only like it if they're hitting the ball badly or already losing their match,' said the professional from long experience. 'That's the only time when they don't mind walking back in with the world watching.'

'Don't worry,' said Phillips easily. 'They said at work that it wasn't important enough to disturb his game. Just to wait and give it to him when he got in.'

Jock Stirling looked curiously at Ned Phillips. 'Lionel Perry's the boss man over at your place, isn't he?'

'Too right, he is,' said Ned, leaning over the counter of the professional's shop and starting to toy absently with a handful of loose tees.

'That's if you're from that big house-building outfit of his, Berebury Homes.' Jock Stirling held the shining club-head out in front of him and studied it critically.

'I am,' said the young man, 'but I've only just joined the firm so I don't really know him – or it – yet.'

'You from away then? I haven't seen you up here before.'

'Too right I am. The North.' He grinned. 'And tennis is my game, anyway.'

'You'll come to golf, then,' said the professional comfortably. 'Later.'

'All in good time,' said Ned Phillips with unimpaired goodwill.

The professional said, 'Your boss'd be a better player if he spent more time up here.'

'Really?' Ned Phillips didn't know that this, too, was one of Jock Stirling's standard remarks.

'But I daresay he's a very busy man these days.' The golf professional gave the club-head a final rub and restored it to a display on the wall. 'Unfortunately by the time most men find out that time's more important than money they're too old to enjoy the game properly.'

'I suppose they feel they've got to make their pile first,' ventured Ned Phillips.

'That's what I mean,' said Jock Stirling, selecting another metal wood from the rack. He grimaced. 'I don't think we need to worry too much about Lionel Perry's pension. The word on the street is that Calleford Construction wants to buy him out and since they say he and his wife are big shareholders in Berebury Homes that shouldn't leave him short of a penny or two.'

'Keen on money, is he?' enquired Ned Phillips negligently.

'Aren't all businessmen?' responded the golf professional, applying the soft cloth to the shining head.

'So they say, so they say.'

'Those I see up here are,' said the professional warmly. 'And all with this fixed idea that time's money. You can't concentrate on your game if you've got one eye on the clock while you're playing.'

'True,' agreed the young man amiably.

The professional turned his glance towards the shop window. 'Looks as if it's a needle match out there. See, they're still fighting it out on the eighteenth.'

'I guess the game isn't over until the fat lady sings,' responded Ned lightly.

'I always say myself that it's not over until the last ball's in the cup,' said Jock Stirling.

'How long does it take them to get round the course?'

'All depends on who's asking,' said the other man.

'How come?'

'If it's their wives that ask then whenever they ring, their hubby is still out on the course,' said Stirling, winking. 'Get it?'

'I'm not married.'

'Then,' advised the older man, 'when you do, whatever you do don't ever tell the little woman when to expect you home. Causes more trouble than you might think, does that.'

'I'll remember that,' promised Phillips. He went on casually, 'So my boss-man hasn't got the time to play better. That it?'

'All your boss is ever after,' remarked Jock Stirling, 'is dry land.'

'Dry land?'

'Land he can buy that's not in the flood plain. For houses. Made the committee here an offer for that patch over there behind the practice tee last year but they wouldn't wear it.'

'Land for building's a bit scarce these days,' offered Ned Phillips. 'Even I know that, but at least they've got Tolmie Park now and there's plenty of ground over there.'

'You don't have to tell me that,' said Jock Stirling tightly. 'Some clever dick had ideas one time about turning the park into one of those pay-and-play golf courses and the old building there into apartments for a Dormyhouse to give the golfers somewhere to stay.'

'Really?' Ned Phillips looked interested. 'How did you feel about that?'

The professional held the club he had been polishing at arms' length and regarded it for a moment before putting it back on the rack and selecting another. 'No skin off my nose if they have an anti-elitist golf course over there. It wouldn't ever have been a proper club like here. You know, with members and a committee and proper competitions and matches. That sort of thing.'

'What happened?'

'Oh, nothing came of it,' said Stirling. 'I expect they were held to ransom by the highwaymen.'

'I don't get it. What highwaymen?'

'Highways authorities, then. The county surveyor and his underlings.' Stirling sniffed. 'The Highways Department always put their oar in on development. If it generates road traffic, then they don't like it and it gets the thumbs down.'

'Waiting for a sweetener?' suggested the young man. 'Or a back-hander?'

The golf professional shrugged his shoulders. 'Who can say? I can't.'

'So what happened at Tolmie Park?'

'The golf project went belly-up and the operator disappeared.'

'Leaving the field wide open for Berebury Homes, I suppose?'

'I wouldn't know about that. I never heard a dicky-bird afterwards about a golf course there.' He resumed his polishing of the club-head. 'I suppose doing anything with it is better than doing nothing.'

'I wouldn't know about that,' said Ned Phillips.

'Then you're not one of those do-good types all against developing the countryside – oh, no, of course you're not. Couldn't work for that outfit if you were, could you?'

'Not easily,' said Ned Phillips.

CHAPTER SEVEN

The next visitor to arrive at Tolmie Park was also female and also wearing a hard hat. There the resemblance to the chubby Melanie Smithers, the conservation officer, ended. This woman was tall and willowy and as far as Detective Inspector Sloan could see under the hard hat, ash blonde. She was wearing white overalls and walked with the panache usually associated with the fashion catwalk.

She swept past Crosby with a winning smile, calmly lifted the tape clearly reading 'POLICE – DO NOT CROSS THIS LINE', and advanced towards Sloan.

'Colleen Murphy,' she murmured in a soft Irish accent. 'Calleshire Fire Service.'

'Ah, miss…that is, madam…' he started to respond as she approached.

'Doctor,' she corrected him sweetly. 'Fire Forensics Investigator.' She gazed at the charred site. 'I'm told Sub-Officer Burton should be around.'

Sloan pointed to Charlie Burton, just coming into sight round a corner of the wrecked part of the building.

'Dear man,' she murmured.

Unclear whether she meant Charlie Burton or himself, Sloan nevertheless felt curiously uplifted.

'Unaccidental fire,' said Burton briefly. 'Window forced on the far side. Slight smell of accelerant when we arrived but you never can tell exactly which one.'

She flashed him a little smile. 'Never. Were there any witnesses?'

'One,' said Burton, 'who has so far chosen to remain anonymous.'

'Dear, dear,' said Dr Murphy. 'That won't do at all. And the building empty, you say?'

'Everyone says so. Waiting for final planning approval, I understand,' said Burton.

Dr Murphy cast her gaze over the jumble of burnt wood and fire-blackened bricks. 'Where would you say the seat of the fire was?'

'Point of origin thought to be in the outer corner of the ballroom here,' replied Burton, jerking a thumb in that direction. 'It's the most damaged part.'

'Furthest away from the main part of the building,' mused Dr Murphy, turning and looking the other way, 'and the double doors leading to the old part, scorched but still closed.'

'Still locked, too,' said Charlie Burton.

'So someone didn't want it to spread too far,' she concluded aloud.

What Detective Inspector Sloan concluded was that brains and beauty could sometimes go together.

'Whether they did or not, we contained it within the hour,' said Burton.

'Well done,' she said absently. 'How long would you say it had been alight before you got here?'

Burton wrinkled his forehead in deep thought. 'Best part of an hour at least.'

'Presumably whoever had set it would want to be sure it had caught,' put in Sloan diffidently, 'before they rang you people.'

He was rewarded with a kindly smile from Dr Murphy. 'That's what we usually find, Inspector.'

Charlie Burton swiftly reasserted himself. 'Then it mushroomed to the ceiling. That's when the roof went.'

'Just for the record,' said Dr Murphy, producing a notebook the size of a powder-compact, 'can you tell me about any fire alarms in this part of the building?'

'There weren't any in use,' said Burton, adding pithily, 'No one to hear them out here if there were.'

'And electricity?'

'Switched off at the mains,' replied Burton. 'First thing we checked.'

Dr Colleen Murphy then proved beyond any doubt that she was a child of her time by asking why the empty building hadn't been vandalised long before now.

Detective Inspector Sloan, a policeman of his time, too, answered that one. 'Gates too securely fastened for a car to get through in the ordinary way.' The fire brigade's bolt cutters would have made short work of them but that was something different. 'And we're really out in the sticks here. Your average yobbo wouldn't fancy walking up the drive here. Too much like hard work.'

'So no car wheel tracks to tell us anything,' she said matter-of-factly. 'Now, were there any casualties?'

'Yes,' said Burton, fire officer.

'No,' said Sloan, detective inspector.

She looked enquiringly from one to the other.

'There were some remains...' said Burton. 'Bones.'

'But thought not to be human,' said Sloan.

'Animal casualties, then?' she said.

'Perhaps,' said Sloan. 'And the pathologist says there were some broken shells – lobster, he thinks – under them.'

She turned and fluttered at him the longest eyelashes Sloan had ever seen. 'Thermidor, you might say.'

'Very probably,' said Detective Inspector Sloan. 'If that means cooked.'

'A tramp's supper?' She raised an elegantly arched eyebrow.

'Possibly.' Sloan hurried on, 'Our local preservation society, though, has a distinctly maverick member. He's given to stunts – anything to raise the profile of an endangered building.'

The finely etched eyebrow went up further still. 'By burning it down?'

'No, no. But perhaps by buying time to assemble opposition. And by planting something like animal bones and shells for us to find to confuse matters.'

'Away from the seat of the fire?' she said, 'to be sure you did find them?'

'Exactly.'

'And sending for us,' put in Burton, putting his oar in with what Sloan considered quite unnecessary vigour, 'just in time for us to find them before the roof falls in.'

'It's been done before,' said Dr Murphy. 'Many times.'

'Dr Dabbe says they'll all have been calcined long before anyone could have got to them,' said Sloan. Dizzy blondes weren't supposed to be so knowledgeable.

'So we'll need a species specific microsatellite marker,' she sighed.

'But Dr Dabbe'll be letting us know all he can,' said Sloan, since as far as he was concerned Dr Murphy might have been speaking in tongues.

'And us, too, all in good time, I'm sure.' She gave both men a dazzling smile. 'Now, what you need to watch out for are two fellows calling themselves loss adjusters and loss assessors. They're like Kilkenny cats together and they'll each want access here before the other and you'll be darlings, won't you, and not let either of them on site until I give the word.'

'Right,' said Burton before Sloan could speak.

'Certainly not,' said Sloan stoutly.

Dr Colleen Murphy turned round and indicated Detective Constable Crosby, still guarding the entrance to the fire-damaged site. 'Now, do you think that the dear boy over there would let my two assistants through that barrier of his? I can see that they've just arrived.'

This time the glow did not extend to Detective Inspector Sloan.

'Well?' said Jeremy Stratton, the planning officer, when Melanie Smithers arrived back, hot and dusty, at the Berebury Council offices. 'Tell me all. Who's done what exactly?'

'Someone's set the Victorian bit alight,' said the conservation officer, wrinkling her nose, 'that's for sure, but I couldn't get near enough to see if the ballroom had been obscuring a cross-wing on the older part.'

He smiled faintly. 'We all have our priorities.'

She flushed. 'Don't be beastly. The fire hadn't got that far anyway.'

'Bad luck.'

'It's all very well for you, Jeremy,' she responded hotly, 'with your one-man crusade to meet all government house-building targets with the least possible bother to all concerned but let me remind you some of us have other things to consider.'

'So presumably had the fire-raiser.'

She frowned. 'That's what's so funny. You see, Berebury Homes aren't planning to do anything they shouldn't for the old house conservation-wise.'

'Bully for them.'

'We haven't had to object to anything in our department.'

'That's suspicious for a start,' he said sarcastically.

'Don't be like that, Jeremy. We've always found them very...well, very cooperative.'

'I should say that makes a change, too.'

'Yes, it does,' she admitted, 'but we at conservation aren't the stumbling block anyway, are we?'

'No,' said Jeremy Stratton immediately, 'but we at planning are. Seeing as it's a greenfield site they want to develop and not one in the local plan. I wouldn't put it past them to argue that the estate is just a garden and therefore a brownfield site.'

Melanie Smithers sighed. 'No, but large brownfield sites aren't all that thick on the ground any longer, more's the pity.'

'You can say that again, my girl.' Jeremy Stratton jerked his thumb in the direction of his own office. 'Every patch of waste land that I can find that isn't in the flood plain has got its new houses...'

'It's awful little boxes,' said the conservation officer.

'...on it already and now the developers' land banks are running low, too.'

'So that only leaves the greenfield bits like Tolmie,' she said, adding without heat 'and by the way I'm not your girl.'

'And the flood plain. Don't forget the flood plain, although it isn't popular with everyone. The insurance companies for starters.'

'Which should make enabling development for Tolmie Park good news all round,' she said.

'But especially for Berebury Homes,' said Jeremy Stratton. 'They wouldn't stand a cat's chance in Hell of building in those grounds otherwise.'

Melanie Smithers might have been young and inexperienced but she wasn't silly.

'Which makes the fire there funnier still, doesn't it?'

CHAPTER EIGHT

'Well, sir,' temporised Detective Inspector Sloan in response to another urgent demand for a progress report from Superintendent Leeyes, 'so far all we've got is a sort of a go-ahead from the fire brigade.'

'Called their dogs off, have they?'

'Not quite, sir, but they've turned their hoses off,' said Sloan.

'Comes to the same thing,' snorted Leeyes.

'Which means that they've more or less left the field free for us.'

'Keep me in the picture, Sloan,' said Leeyes. 'I'll be in my office.'

Resisting a strong impulse to respond to this, too, Sloan turned back to the fire officer at his side. 'You were saying…'

'That there's one thing I can tell you for free,' said Charlie Burton as Dr Murphy went over to greet her assistants.

Sloan maintained a commendable silence. He wanted to know more than one thing, much more.

'And that's that we were meant to put this fire out before it had spread too far,' said Charlie Burton.

This was something that Sloan had already worked out for himself. So, no doubt, had Dr Murphy.

'If,' said Burton, 'we hadn't had that three nines call from the telephone box the whole place would have gone up in smoke before anyone knew there was a fire there.'

'Talking of smoke,' said Sloan, 'surely that would have been seen from the road sooner or later?'

'You must be joking,' said the fire officer. 'No one would have seen anything from the road until the building here was practically a burnt-out wreck.'

'Which, oddly enough,' murmured Sloan pensively, half to himself, 'doesn't seem to have been what the arsonist had in mind.'

Charlie Burton jerked a thumb. 'Remember, when that pile was built the distance from the gate to the house was what mattered to snobs like the Filligrees. The longer the better if you wanted to keep up with the Joneses.'

'You knew them, did you?' said Sloan, straight-faced.

'Not exactly,' said the fire officer, shaking his head, 'but my wife's granny was a skivvy there when she was a girl. Before the war.'

'What happened to them?'

'Dunno. Died out, I expect.' He pushed his helmet back on his forehead. 'She used to talk about the grand parties they had there in the old days, although she's really lost it mentally now. All the maids would have new outfits for a really big do.'

'Other times, other days,' said Sloan absently. 'Tell me, does this fire have any of the hallmarks of an insurance job to you?'

The fire officer shook his head again. 'The place was empty, wasn't it? Not full of antique furniture or anything like that. And that doesn't explain the heap of bones or why they're sitting on what looks like a heap of old bits of seashell.'

'Nothing,' declared Sloan fervently, 'explains either.'

'Now who's coming?' grumbled Detective Constable Crosby as Dr Colleen Murphy's two assistants hastened to her side. He was looking back down the drive to the point where it joined the road to Tolmie. 'If anyone else turns up we'll have to start a queue.'

'You're a long way from being into crowd control,' said Sloan with some asperity. 'And never forget, Crosby,' he added, quoting his old Station Sergeant and early mentor, 'interested parties are always of interest in any police investigation.' He wouldn't be surprised if that applied to arson, too.

In spades.

Had there been any doubt about whether Randolph Mansfield, architect, and Derek Hitchin, project manager, were interested parties, they very soon dispelled it.

'We shall need to brief the insurance assessors,' began Mansfield.

'And see whether we need to get the structural engineers in...' chimed in Hitchin.

'The safety aspect, too...' said Mansfield. 'That comes into it.'

'And see where we shall need to deploy our resources...' Hitchin was already peering round the site.

'Conservation area...' That was the architect.

'Planning people...' That was the project manager.

'But safety comes first,' said Randolph Mansfield.

'I'm sure it does,' said Detective Inspector Sloan, 'but our investigations take priority and everything else will have to wait.' From where he stood he could see Dr Murphy and her assistants hard at work.

'And, of course, we need to brief our boss on the extent of the damage,' said Hitchin. 'As soon as possible.'

Detective Inspector Sloan sighed. The person he had to brief was Superintendent Leeyes, sitting like a waiting spider at the centre of a web. When it came to deploying his own meagre resources the way ahead was less clear. In theory, police reinforcements should be being summoned as of now but they shouldn't be called out at all just for a case of arson already being investigated and a possible prank.

'The development here is of great importance for the economy of this part of Calleshire,' said Mansfield in the high-handed tone he used for everyone who wasn't either an architect or a client. Actually some clients got the high-handed tone, too, should they show signs of wanting their own way and not his.

Detective Inspector Sloan sighed again. If there was one thing that wasn't the concern of the constabulary, it was the economy.

Derek Hitchin was taking a great interest in the burnt-out shell of the billiard room. 'Thank God we've got the drawings.'

'What drawings?' said Sloan.

'Architectural ones.' Hitchin nodded in the direction of the building. 'We had to have a full survey done when we applied for Listed Building Consent, didn't we, Randolph?'

'We did. Delay will be a factor when it comes to restoration, though,' said Mansfield.

'If it does, that is,' said Hitchin. 'The planning officer may look kindly on the demolition of this section, although if you were to ask me I would say that repairing this wreck shouldn't be too difficult.'

Randolph Mansfield turned to Sloan. 'Delay, Inspector, is the biggest weapon in the armoury of the local authority.'

'And time's money,' said Hitchin.

Sloan, professionally interested in weapons, considered this one – delay – with detachment. Who wielded the weapon could be important, too. Even now. Then there was the old Viking tradition that whoever removed a weapon from a death wound was obliged to avenge it. He turned back from this intriguing thought to look at the bare bones of the damaged building, such rafters as remained looking for all the world like ribs. He gave the two men from Berebury Homes a long look and said, 'But you will understand that as far as our investigations go, gentlemen, your money and your time don't come into the equation.'

There was something surprisingly satisfying, decided Detective Inspector Sloan, about sitting back in his own chair in his own office. He found he relished it. He pulled his chair up to the desk – his desk – and drew his in-tray towards him. There was the usual pile of routine communications waiting for his attention but, sifting quickly through the dross, he found the one that he was looking for: the message from the Greatorex Museum.

It was from Hilary Collins and was accompanied by a

printed copy of the museum's thumbnail photograph of the missing portrait of Sir Francis Filligree. Sloan studied the picture before handing it over to Detective Constable Crosby. 'Get that blown up, will you, Crosby? As big an enlargement as you can.'

The constable gave it a cursory glance. 'Wouldn't have thought that was worth stealing myself, would you, sir?'

'Somebody did,' said Sloan briefly.

'But,' persisted Crosby, 'what would you want to steal something like that for?'

'Money, maybe,' said Sloan, adding slowly, 'Or maybe not.'

'Not my money,' said Crosby firmly.

'Or the view, perhaps.' The constable's money, Sloan knew, went on taking advanced driving courses.

Crosby screwed up his eyes. 'There isn't much of that in the picture apart from the man and his wife. Just some trees in the long grass and the house.'

'And a particular view of the house that isn't visible anymore. That's what the lady at the museum said. A view of great interest to the conservation officer at the council, too, and a view of a house where there has been a mysterious fire. As for the rest, Crosby, we don't know yet,' said Sloan, adding absently, 'but we will one day.'

'There's something else that's a bit funny, sir,' said Crosby. 'There's someone in the frame who wants to buy the place…'

'While it's still smouldering is a bit soon for a fire sale to be on the cards,' murmured Sloan ironically.

'He says he wanted to buy it before the fire,' said Crosby. 'And he says he wrote to Berebury Homes to tell them so.'

'That's different,' said Sloan more alertly. 'What does he want it for? Building twice as many houses on site as all the others?'

'He didn't say.'

'Check him out, Crosby. Money laundering can take some strange forms.' So, he sighed, did the transactional fraud on which he should be working this minute.

Crosby was still looking at the museum's reproduction of the portrait. 'Looks as if Sir Francis might have been a bit of a lad to me. He's a redhead for a start and they usually cause trouble.' He tilted it to the light and took another look. 'With an eye for the ladies, I should say. That's a pretty little wife beside him.'

'I think the artist – any artist – would have seen to that,' said Detective Inspector Sloan. 'Probably wouldn't have got paid if he hadn't and for your information, Crosby, it's known as artistic licence.'

Crosby swept the photograph into a document case. 'One thing you can say for the camera is that it never lies.'

Reminding himself to have a little chat later with the detective constable on the subject of evidence as it related to digital photography, Sloan said, 'And when you've seen to the photograph you can find out as much as you can about Sir Francis.'

'But he's been dead for the best part of two hundred years,' protested Crosby. 'Or is it three?'

'Since Nelson lost his eye, anyway,' agreed Sloan, 'but it's not a crime to set light to animal bones and pile them on crushed shells and unless there's definitely been arson out at

Tolmie Park, the theft of the portrait and the damage to the display cabinet in the museum are the only offences we've got to go on.' He pointed to Hilary Collins' note. 'She says they're still running through their records of the Anglo-Saxon artefacts in their keeping at the museum.'

'Sounds painful,' commented Crosby.

'To see if anything's missing from their collection,' said Sloan repressively.

'I can't see anyone wanting to steal bits and pieces like that, either,' said Crosby.

'And while you're seeing to the Filligree family history,' went on Sloan, who had now thought of at least one reason why the Anglo-Saxon pieces could have been taken from the museum, 'I'm going to try to get hold of an animal osteologist.'

'Beg pardon, sir?'

Detective Inspector Sloan sighed. 'An expert on non-human bones. There'll be one at the university. Bound to be.' He wasn't quite as sure of this as he would once have been, media studies seeming to have overtaken the sciences, pure and applied.

'I would have thought a butcher would do.' Crosby sniffed.

'Very probably but I must remind you, Crosby, that the Courts prefer expert witnesses.' The fact that the superintendent held them in the deepest distrust, he felt was better kept from the constable's young ears.

'Or a vet,' said Crosby mulishly.

As far as Sloan was concerned he was willing to accept the great interest evinced by the police sniffer dog on site as incontrovertible evidence although he didn't suppose any Court would.

'What you want, Crosby,' said Sloan neatly, 'is not a vet but a Baronetage. And when you've found one, we're going round to the bank.'

CHAPTER NINE

The Calleshire and Counties Bank maintained their head office in the county town of Calleford. The fine Regency building, situated practically in the shadow of the old minster there, projected respectability and stability at every turn. Its mahogany counters were positioned on a chequered marble floor, whilst the tellers were dressed soberly enough to satisfy the oldest and crustiest – and once upon time, the wealthiest – of their customers.

Nowadays, as Sloan would have been the first to agree, some of the young could be very wealthy indeed: pop musicians and footballers, mostly. And some of the young who weren't very wealthy behaved as arrogantly as if they were – which was buying trouble, for them as well as for the police.

'We have an appointment with the manager,' announced Detective Inspector Sloan, pleased to note that the credentials of the two policemen were politely but efficiently inspected. He was not – had never been – taken in by marble and mahogany or the many ways of giving the illusion of honesty, not even by elegant brochures and thick writing paper, still less by names on the board.

'If you will come this way, gentlemen, please,' said a well-trained minion.

Sloan was happy to see, though, looking round, that the Calleshire and Counties Bank had state of the art security protection against robbery.

Not, though, it soon transpired, against fraud.

'Our connection with Tolmie Park?' Douglas Anderson's face assumed a regretful expression. 'Most unfortunate.' He sighed. 'Something I'm afraid in the end we had to write off to experience.'

'Write off, anyway,' offered Crosby inelegantly.

'Indeed,' agreed the manager. 'I'm afraid we have been given to understand that the borrower concerned is living in considerable comfort in a country which has no extradition treaties with the United Kingdom.'

'Galling,' said Detective Inspector Sloan.

'We all make mistakes,' said Anderson. He coughed. 'I must say I considered that the board took a very magnanimous view in the circumstances.'

Magnanimity as a response to failure was not the usual reward down at the police station. Higher ranks didn't like failure and the press enjoyed a field day and if there was an official enquiry then it was the deputy-heads that rolled.

'But then,' added the manager shrewdly, 'most of the board knew the gentleman in question themselves.'

'Ah,' said Sloan. That would have helped.

'It's not what you know, but who you know,' observed Detective Constable Crosby, who cherished the notion that this was why he had not progressed further up the promotion ladder.

'Golf club,' said the manager succinctly. 'He was practically scratch, I understand. Actually, that did have some bearing on the circumstances.'

'Circumstances alter cases,' put in Crosby sententiously.

'The particular circumstance in this case was that the – er – defaulter intended to…' the bank manager swiftly amended this, 'told us that he intended – to open a golf course there.'

Detective Inspector Sloan nodded. 'Quite a good use for the house and land.'

'That was what my board thought, too,' said the banker.

'So you were halfway there,' said Crosby, 'weren't you?'

'True but in this line of country we all get our fingers burnt from time to time,' said the manager philosophically. 'They told me to cut our losses as soon as I possibly could.'

'Fire sale,' pronounced Crosby knowledgeably.

The manager looked at the constable curiously. 'Only in a manner of speaking. We still had the deeds – we'd kept them as surety for the loan for buying the estate and fortunately had only advanced the extra funds for the proposed development.'

'That would have been a help towards balancing the books,' murmured Sloan, resisting the temptation to say that half a loaf was better than no bread.

The manager moved a pile of papers on his desk fractionally to one side before saying, 'So we were able to sell the estate ourselves and recoup half the loan.'

'And keep quiet about the other half,' pointed out Crosby unkindly.

'It wouldn't have done the bank any good to go public,' said the manager.

'That's true,' said Sloan. He could see that it would have upset the illusion of security engendered by all that marble and mahogany, but he did not say so.

'That was the board's view, anyway, when I put it to them,'

said Douglas Anderson a trifle defensively. 'In fact one of them even quoted an Italian proverb to me – *tutti possono sbagliare*.'

'Tut tut what?' asked Crosby.

'It means, "We can all make mistakes",' translated the bank manager.

Detective Inspector Sloan envied him. Those holding the office of constable didn't have any board behind which to shelter. The responsibilities were theirs and theirs alone whatever their rank. It sounded to him rather as if the board had taken the decision to keep quiet unto themselves. Perhaps, like Sloan, they had all been unduly influenced when young by those lines in Rudyard Kipling's poem "If" about not breathing a word about their loss.

'So, gentlemen, you will understand why we were very happy to sell Tolmie Park in its existing condition…'

'As was,' put in Crosby.

'*Caveat emptor*,' murmured Sloan in Latin. It didn't need translating but he did it all the same. 'Buyer beware.'

'…to Berebury Homes, to help towards recouping our losses,' said Douglas Anderson. 'And let them take a punt on getting planning permission. After all they're long-standing customers of ours with a good reputation in these parts.'

To sell to them for a song, concluded Detective Inspector Sloan.

But silently.

Auriole Allen was waiting for Ned Phillips when he got back to the offices of Berebury Homes from the golf club. 'How did he take it?'

'The boss? Oh, all right, I suppose.' Ned Phillips grimaced.

'He wasn't best pleased, naturally.'

She gave him a sharp look. 'Naturally.'

'Mr Perry's bound to be a bit upset, isn't he?' said Phillips. 'After all, a fire doesn't usually help anything.'

Auriole Allen, the press and public relations specialist, said heavily, 'Whatever actually happened, I can assure you, Ned, that there are plenty of people out there ready and waiting to put the worst possible construction on a fire in a house when there's building work in the offing. Whichever way you look at it, a fire can't be good news.'

'Which is presumably what somebody had in mind when they started it.' He gave her a bland smile. 'Or have I got that wrong?'

'It's certainly going to hold up any development,' she said.

'But not for long, I hope.'

'Who knows?' she said enigmatically. 'The conservation people are quite capable of asking for a completely revised application and that can take forever.'

Ned Phillips reached back into his car for his jacket. 'Could it be meant as a warning shot across the bows?'

'About what?'

'The development over there.'

She shook her head. 'The only written objection that's come in has been from the Berebury Preservation Society and that doesn't mean a lot because they object to everything on principle.'

The young man shrugged himself into his jacket. 'Then there's Calleford Construction sniffing around for a takeover, or so I've heard.'

She narrowed her eyes. 'And how did you hear about that? You're supposed to be new here.'

'At the golf club,' he said.

'Talking of the golf club, is Mr Perry going over to Tolmie first?' she asked. 'Derek and Randolph are on their way there now.'

'Nope, he's coming straight back here.'

She let out an audible sigh of relief. 'That's good. I'm working on a press release now by way of damage limitation and I'd like to run it past him.'

'Better safe than sorry, Mrs Allen.'

Suspecting irony, she said 'Talking of safe, how come you're back here ahead of him?'

'I took a short cut through the woods.'

Her head came up. 'I thought you were a stranger to Berebury. You said you were.'

He flashed an impish grin in her direction and threw up his hands. 'All right, I give in. You win. It's just that I'm quicker on the road. I've got youth on my side and all that.'

She cast her eyes in the direction of the vehicle he had been driving and said drily, 'And a fast car.'

After Ned Phillips had gone on his way Auriole Allen sat for a minute or two at her desk, scribbling some notes. Then she picked up her telephone and dialled Robert Selby's office extension. 'Robert,' she said, 'I'm beginning to wonder about that omniscient young man who's just joined us…your new assistant.'

'You mean Ned Phillips?' said Robert Selby directly. He was only deliberately obfuscating when it came to figures that he didn't want anyone else to understand.

'Yes, I do mean him. Well, he knows about this takeover

offer we've had for Tolmie Park from Calleford Construction
and says he heard about it at the golf club.'

'Which offer?' the finance director asked. 'There were two,
don't forget.'

'Oh, yes…' her voice faltered. 'I'd forgotten about that man
who wrote to us this morning.'

'I hadn't,' said Selby pointedly.

'Ned Phillips was talking about the Calleford Construction
people, at least,' she paused, 'that's what he said.'

'It would have been more of a help if it had been from the
other man – the one called Stuart Bellamy,' said Robert Selby.
'We might have got to know a bit more about him if it had.
We could do with a handle on our Mr Bellamy, whoever he
is.'

'And I could do without a fire to have to deny Berebury
Homes starting. I know that's not good English but you know
what I mean,' she said, squinting down at her notes. 'No one's
going to believe us.'

'Has anyone said that we did start it?'

'Not yet, Robert, but they will. As soon as the police get
round to asking who benefits. It's only us.'

'Now that's just where you're wrong, Auriole. Should they
ever get to take us over, God forbid, Calleford Construction
stand to be quite considerable beneficiaries of Tolmie Park
being burnt to the ground, too.'

She raised her elegantly arched eyebrows. 'Too?'

'Too. Remember, they only want the land, just as we do.
Not an elegant ruin with a big repair bill supervised by all the
conservation and heritage people in the country.'

She sighed. 'I suppose you're right.'

'And as for this Mr Stuart Bellamy...' he said.

'Yes?'

'Who knows what he wants Tolmie Park for – I don't – but I can tell you one thing about Stuart Bellamy and that's that he can afford to buy it.'

'That's interesting,' she said. 'How do you know?'

'The fellow gave us the name of his bank so that we could check that he was genuine and, guess what, he's with the same bank as we are. When I ran his name past the Calleshire and Counties Bank chap, Douglas Anderson, he told me that though he couldn't tell me anything about him...'

'Professional ethics,' said Auriole immediately. 'It's a well-known get-out if the press are chasing you and one there's no other way round.'

'But,' went on the finance director, 'what the bank manager told me he could do for Berebury Homes was assure me that Bellamy wouldn't even need to borrow to pay for it. Apparently Bellamy had given his permission for us to be told as much.'

'No money worries on the Bellamy front, then?' Auriole Allen drew those arched eyebrows together in an expression of puzzlement. 'That makes a change in this day and age, doesn't it?'

'Exactly,' said Robert Selby, 'and in my experience that's always interesting in itself. Very. It makes you think, too.'

'Does Lionel know all this?'

'Not yet, but he soon will. As soon as I can get hold of him.'

* * *

'Jonathon,' bawled a girl over the steady background hum of machinery at the works of Berebury Precision Engineering out on the Luston road, 'you're wanted in the front office.' When there was no immediate response to this she added even more loudly and with evident satisfaction, 'By the police.'

That did the trick.

A door opened and an untidy young man in a white coat appeared. 'And what is it I'm wanted for?' he asked the two policemen waiting there truculently.

'We'd just like a little help with our enquiries,' said Detective Inspector Sloan blandly.

'You ought to get yourselves a new record,' said Jonathon Ayling. 'That one's practically worn out. And whatever it is you're trying to pin on me, I didn't do it.'

'Good,' said Detective Inspector Sloan briskly, 'but we'd still like a chat about the fire at Tolmie Park.'

'I might have guessed,' he sounded resigned. 'The Preservation Society hauled me over to one of their precious meetings in my lunch-hour and grilled me about it. I didn't get any lunch.'

'Neither did I,' said Crosby plaintively.

Jonathon Ayling ignored this. 'And no, for your information I didn't set the fire there.'

'Then you won't mind our asking you about your movements this morning, will you?' said Sloan, taking out his notebook.

'I mind you trying to pin something on me that I didn't do,' said Ayling heatedly. 'I'm a preservationist, not a fire-raiser, and you don't preserve buildings by burning them down.'

'Not usually,' said Sloan.

Suddenly Jonathon Ayling relaxed. 'But I grant you, investigations tend to delay developments.'

'That had occurred to us,' said Sloan, although he wasn't at all sure that the thought had crossed Crosby's mind.

Ayling said, 'Give Berebury Council's planning officer, Jeremy Stratton, half a chance and you bet he'll put off making any recommendation to his precious committee as long as he can and they can't decide until he does.'

'Would he by any chance have been the man whose face was painted on your balloon earlier this year?' asked Sloan. The police had been called in when the biggest rubber balloon ever seen in the village of Cullingoak had been blown up by the forge's bellows and attracted a crowd deemed in need of control, that is until someone stuck a pin in it and it shrivelled to nothing with an eerie squeal.

Ayling grinned. 'I'll say. It was a beautiful old forge and our God-awful planning officer recommended that permission be given for it all to be dismantled so that some fat cat could build a block of flats on the site.' He gave Sloan a very straight look indeed and added, 'And if you were to ask me why, I couldn't say I'm sure. He's normally a right antediluvian.'

'So,' said Sloan, sticking to the point but all the same tucking Ayling's unspoken implication into his mind for further consideration at a later time, 'what exactly were your movements this morning?'

'I had a bit of breakfast at Bellini's over the road then I clocked in at the grindstone here as usual at eight o'clock, checked all our electronic gear and computer settings, micrometers now being a thing of the past, chatted with the bloke in charge of future orders and then headed out to deliver some custom-built burglar alarms for Calleshire Construction.'

'Ah,' said Detective Constable Crosby, looking interested for the first time. The mental road-map of the county of Calleshire was one thing that was clear in his mind. 'That's out beyond Tolmie.'

'Aren't our policemen wonderful?' marvelled Ayling.

'So you went past Tolmie Park this morning?' said Sloan.

'Twice, actually,' said Ayling solemnly. 'There and back.'

'On business?'

'I can assure you that nobody in their right mind goes to see the firm of Calleford Construction Ltd for pleasure.' He gave a disparaging sniff. 'The rotters were complaining about some work we'd done for them here.' Jonathon Ayling waved a hand to encompass the building behind them from which the steady hum of machinery could still be heard.

'And what do you do here?' asked Sloan curiously.

'Manufacture really minute parts for other manufacturers or, as Jonathon Swift put it so well, "A flea hath smaller fleas that on him prey; and these have smaller fleas to bite 'em, and so proceed ad infinitum".' He gave a wry grin. 'You might say that we at Berebury Precision Engineering are the smallest fleas of all. The bottom of the heap.'

'Skilled, though, all the same,' said Sloan appreciatively. Policing wasn't precise.

'Skill without imagination is mere craftsmanship,' said Jonathon Ayling cynically. 'It's skill with imagination that makes art. We just make tiny bits and pieces for companies like Calleford Construction, God rest their souls – except that I doubt if they have them.'

'Have what?' asked Crosby, somewhat bewildered.

'Souls,' spat out Jonathon Ayling. 'We make what they

want to their own specifications, like very, very small usually. Only this time they say we didn't.'

'Didn't what?' asked Crosby.

Jonathon Ayling said, 'Make it to their precise specification. At least that's what they insist. If you ask me, all they really want to do is delay paying us. And if it's of any interest to you the bloke I saw there was their works manager.' He stopped, struck by a sudden thought. 'If you do catch your arsonist you might send him out to Calleford Construction. Their outfit could do with a good fire. Nineteen-sixties architecture at its very worst. It's enough to make you see why we get passionate about saving buildings like Tolmie Park.'

'And last night?' said Sloan, unmoved by this. 'What did you do after work yesterday?'

Jonathon Ayling cocked his head on one side. 'So the two gentlemen are interested in all my movements, are they?'

'Just those after you left work yesterday,' said Sloan. Crosby gave no sign of interest whatsoever.

'I didn't get to leave this sweatshop until after seven,' said Ayling, 'and I made for The Claviger's Arms over at Almstone. As pubs go, it's quite good. Had a bite and a few jars there and eventually went home.'

'Alone?'

He gave a mocking sob. 'Home alone, Inspector.'

'By car?' said Sloan unamused.

'Sure. It's nearly as clapped-out as I am these days but it still goes.'

Detective Inspector Sloan pointed to Ayling's footwear. 'Are these yesterday's shoes?'

'And today's. I don't sleep in them though.'

Sloan produced a sealable plastic bag and some slippers. 'What I would like to do is to take your shoes away to let our people have a look at them. I'm sure you won't have any objection to that, now, will you?'

If Jonathon Ayling did have any objection, he wasn't saying, but his self confidence visibly oozed away, deflating not unlike the pricked balloon on the bellows at the forge at Cullingoak.

CHAPTER TEN

Behind the scenes at the Greatorex Museum, Hilary Collins produced the results of her researches. She had clearly been beavering away in their archives. 'As far as I can establish so far, Inspector, the Filligree family left England before the Second World War – that is in the middle of the nineteen-thirties for – Switzerland.'

'Running away?' suggested Detective Constable Crosby, a young man brought up on a diet of war films. 'Or dodging conscription?'

She shook her head. 'Neither. I understand that the then owner of Tolmie Park – Sir Edward Filligree – was at one time in the Territorials but was found to be suffering from tuberculosis and invalided out. He was sent to a sanatorium in Switzerland for his health.'

'The White Plague,' said Detective Inspector Sloan. 'There was a lot of it about then.'

Hilary Collins said, 'Both the house at Tolmie and the land there were sold and it seems very little was heard from him after that.'

'There was a war on,' said Crosby, echoing a lot of film dialogue.

'Exactly,' she said. 'Whilst I am sure some mail got through it wouldn't have been easy for him to keep in touch with Calleshire during hostilities.'

'Perhaps he wanted to shake the dust of the old country off his feet,' said Crosby, who had also watched every film there ever was about the French Foreign Legion.

'Possibly.' Hilary Collins sounded doubtful.

'Perhaps he died there, then,' suggested Crosby. 'People often died of tuberculosis, didn't they?'

'People only die once,' Sloan corrected him crisply. 'Not often.'

Hilary Collins hurried on. 'The house was requisitioned – that is to say, commandeered – by the Army, which didn't do a lot for it or for the trees in the park.'

'Firewood?' groaned Sloan, a great garden man himself.

'Tanks on the lawn?' said Crosby.

'Very probably,' said Hilary Collins to both suggestions. 'In any case the family would not have been rich by the time the house came to be sold. They'd lost almost everything by then.'

'Gambling?' suggested Sloan.

'Death duties,' said the museum assistant repressively. 'They called them fines in the old days, which I suppose is what they are.'

'Punishment for dying?' Crosby sounded astonished.

'In medieval times they were a form of compensation to the Crown for the loss of an adult male worker,' said Hilary Collins.

'The good old days, Crosby, let me remind you,' said Sloan. 'Now, miss, can you tell us something about this wild club his ancestors belonged to? The Crustaceans, I think you said it was called.'

She pursed her lips. 'I don't know exactly what sort of

goings-on they went in for, Inspector, but I do know they had a very bad reputation locally at the time. I expect they were pure braggadocios, and proud of it.'

'Impure, probably,' put in Crosby automatically, not having met the word before.

'High jinks, anyway,' said Hilary Collins. 'Playing card games for very high stakes, that sort of thing.'

'Dicing with death,' said Crosby, who wasn't above cutting a corner on the high road himself, betting the ranch on there being no one coming the other way.

'Young men like taking risks,' said Sloan, who had often suffered bruises when trying to stop them. 'Hence Russian roulette.'

Hilary Collins, spinster, gave both men a look of total lack of understanding. 'Think of their poor wives and children! Riches to rags at the throw of a dice or the turn of a card. Disgraceful.'

'Rites of passage are common to all tribes,' said Sloan. That had come straight from the lips of one of the unfortunate lecturers at adult education classes attended by Superintendent Leeyes. The sentiment hadn't gone down at all well with the superintendent.

'If that's what you call wagering everything you owned on barouche racing down the drive at Tolmie Park...' began Hilary Collins, who obviously wasn't struck on the idea of rites of passage either.

'Nothing changes,' said Detective Inspector Sloan. Even now there were bikers using the common over at Cullingoak for purposes for which it had not been intended, no doubt with bets on the side.

'Showing off is what I call it,' said the museum assistant unsympathetically. 'Think of the horses.'

Detective Inspector Sloan, who had learnt from an older generation that as a matter of good practice it was as well not to do anything to frighten the horses, let alone the magistrates, merely said, 'Quite so, miss. So, tell me, where does the Crustacean bit come in?'

'It was their – well, sort of trademark,' she said. 'They used to eat lobsters at their dinners and scatter the shells wherever they went.' She looked disapproving. 'Especially when they'd been up to no good. Then,' she said with lemon lips, 'there were their masked balls…'

'Dangerous,' agreed Sloan without hesitation. Masked balls weren't quite as dangerous for a young woman, in his opinion, as walking home unescorted down a remote country lane at two o'clock in the morning, but still dangerous. Knowing thine enemy – as the ancients had it – was important. The fact that this wasn't always easy in the detective branch either, he kept to himself. Instead he said to Hilary Collins, 'Now, miss, about your Anglo-Saxon artefacts…'

'It's about the Anglo-Saxon items taken from the museum, sir,' began Sloan as he and Crosby walked into Superintendent Leeyes' office in Berebury Police Station.

'Stolen from the museum, you mean, Sloan.' The superintendent was not a man to mince his words.

'Missing, anyway,' said Sloan. That was as far as he was prepared to go for the time being.

'Not there,' contributed Detective Constable Crosby helpfully.

Leeyes glared across his desk at his two subordinates. 'Well?'

'Not a great deal more to say about them at this stage, sir, I'm afraid.' Duty bound, Sloan had reported back to the superintendent in Berebury as soon as he could. 'It would seem,' he went on carefully, 'that the items that aren't there were small pieces of no great intrinsic value.'

'In theft, Sloan,' thundered the superintendent, sounding very like Lady Bracknell, 'the value of the goods taken is immaterial. Let me remind you that there are no such things as unconsidered trifles in police work.'

'Quite so, sir,' said Sloan, 'but in my opinion the significant thing in this instance is that items of greater – much greater – value in the same display cabinet were left and we know that the thief was undisturbed and didn't have to leave in a hurry.'

Detective Constable Crosby flicked his notebook open and began to read. 'The famous Almstone Brooch is still there…at least,' he added dubiously, 'Hilary Collins says it's famous.'

'Jewelled,' put in Sloan. 'Found by Professor Michael Ripley and part of the Almstone hoard which he excavated – and still there in the display cabinet.'

'A quoit brooch,' went on Crosby. 'And some gold bracteates.'

'A wafer-thin leaf of metal,' explained Sloan swiftly, before the superintendent could draw breath, 'used in the manufacture of embossed pendants.'

'Still there,' chimed in Crosby. 'That is, not taken. Also a sword-hilt with silver and niello inlay…'

Sloan had seen a piece there that could have come straight

from his wife's dressing-table – a garnet brooch of cast silver. Perhaps nothing changed...

'Suppose you just tell me what isn't there,' suggested Leeyes.

'Just some small bronze pins and a type of button, sir. Oh, and some little pieces of bone...'

The superintendent's head came up on the instant. 'Bone?'

'There was nothing missing from the Paleolithic Room, sir,' said Sloan hastily. 'The auroch remains are still there.'

The superintendent subsided back in his seat.

'Nothing else appears be missing from that cabinet, sir, not even some fragments of reindeer antlers thought to have been used until recently in the Cullingoak Horn Dance. They've been carbon-dated to before the Norman Conquest.'

'Nothing of monetary value taken, you say,' murmured Leeyes thoughtfully. 'But perhaps worth someone's while to break in and take them all the same, would you say?'

'The display cabinet might just have broken under the weight of whoever took the portrait, sir.'

Superintendent Leeyes leant back in his chair. 'So, what we have so far is a case of arson...

'The fire people think so,' said Sloan.

'And one definite case of theft,' the superintendent ticked off his fingers. 'A portrait of undoubtedly some – but not startling – value and one doubtful case of theft: a handful of Anglo-Saxon artefacts presumably of no commercial value at all that may have merely gone missing in the break-in...'

Detective Inspector Sloan pointed in the direction of Crosby's notebook. 'I'm not entirely sure about that yet, sir.'

'On the police principle of everything having its price?' enquired the superintendent, quite mildly for him.

'On the presumption that there was a reason for the theft or thefts,' said Sloan. He coughed. 'There is also, sir, a fairly strong rumour going the rounds, which may or may not be relevant, that the firm of Calleford Construction has it in mind to take over Berebury Homes.'

The superintendent considered this. 'So they have a fire with a view to hitting a man when he's down?'

'It's easier,' said Sloan. Sportsmanship was not to be presumed in police work.

'No smoke without fire,' observed Crosby from the sidelines.

Superintendent Leeyes favoured Crosby with a baleful look. 'Arson is one thing, constable. Bones are quite another.'

'Now thought to be animal ones,' interposed Sloan. He thought it better not to mention the supporting evidence of the sniffer dog. 'The remains have gone to forensics and they're being examined now. As have the shells they were sitting on. Lobster ones, almost certainly.'

'So we don't know why the portrait and the other bits and pieces were stolen from the museum, or why the fire was set or why some bones were left sitting on the floor on some old shells when it was lit. That right, Sloan?'

'Yes, sir.'

'You haven't got very far, have you?'

'Jonathon Ayling's shoes are a bit suspect,' said Sloan, deciding to neither apologise nor explain. 'They've gone to forensics, as well.'

The superintendent steepled his fingers, 'That apart, I think we can have what you might call an educated guess about the lobster shells, can't we?'

'I think so. Someone somewhere wants the connection made between the missing portrait and Tolmie Park,' said Detective Inspector Sloan.

'But by whom? Tell me that, Sloan.'

'I'm seeing another interested party next, sir. Berebury Homes. They must come into this somewhere but I don't know where yet.'

Superintendent Leeyes growled, 'In my time in the force I think I've seen every crime in the book except Morris dancing but there's something going on here that even I don't understand.'

'Me neither,' said Sloan – but under his breath.

Detective Constable Crosby consulted a street map and then counted the numbers down from the junction until he came to the fourth house on his left. He stopped the car in front of a neat detached dwelling half way down a road comprised of similar small and neat detached dwellings. There was nothing to distinguish number 8, Acacia Avenue from any of its neighbours in what was essentially a very ordinary road but it was, he hoped, the home of Stuart Bellamy.

As far as Crosby was concerned it did not look like a house at which seven figure cheques would be written as a matter of course – and seven figures was what he had been told Tolmie Park would be worth with planning permission. What it was worth without planning permission was something no one was prepared to tell him. 'It might even be a white elephant,' was what Detective Inspector Sloan had said as he had sped him on his way. 'A downright liability, I would have thought, Crosby, except that this Stuart Bellamy, whoever he is, wants to buy it whatever it's like.'

And if that wasn't suspicious, then Crosby didn't know what was. He approached the front door, noting that the car parked in the drive was the same one that had been at Tolmie Park during the fire. With a bit of luck, its owner should be at home.

He was.

Moreover, Stuart Bellamy recognised Crosby from the scene of the fire. 'Come in,' he said, leading the way to the sitting room.

'Just checking on one or two little matters, sir,' Crosby began his spiel.

'Sure,' said Bellamy easily.

'We gather that you're interested in buying Tolmie Park,' said Crosby.

'Not a crime,' said Bellamy.

'No, sir, that's very true, but as you were there at the time of the fire...'

'Not a crime either,' pointed out Bellamy. 'Or is it?'

'No, not in itself,' agreed Crosby, forbearing to add what he had been taught during his training about those who cause a fire often being among the crowd watching it, 'but as the fire was almost certainly a crime scene...'

'Arson, I thought it was called,' supplied Bellamy pithily. 'But as you must appreciate, I wanted to buy it, not burn it to the ground.'

'Tolmie Park could well be worth more burnt to the

ground,' said Crosby, who had had this spelt out to him by Inspector Sloan.

'Very possibly, but as it happens should that have been the case, Constable, then I wouldn't have wished to buy it.'

'Might I therefore ask,' enquired Crosby delicately, 'for what purpose you do wish to buy it?' He allowed his glance to encompass the décor of number 8's sitting room in which chintz figured prominently: the carpet was good without being outstanding, the wallpaper attractive but understated.

Stuart Bellamy waved a hand. 'Seeing as you ask, Constable, and seeing that we're not yet quite a police state, I can tell you that it is being bought for residential purposes. You know, to live in.'

'That's what we'd heard, sir.' The two vases on the mantelpiece would have fitted in at Tolmie Park all right but the scale of the furniture was definitely more Acacia Avenue than any old and stately home.

Bellamy's head came up on the instant. 'Heard from whom?'

'A gentleman called Lionel Perry whose firm owns it at the moment. He told us you wanted to make him an offer. I take it, sir, that it wasn't an offer he couldn't refuse?'

'As a matter of fact, Constable, he did refuse it without even telling us what he would take for the place.'

'Us?' Detective Constable Crosby pounced on the word.

'I was making enquiries on behalf of myself and another,' said Bellamy smoothly.

'I think that's what Mr Perry was afraid of,' said the detective constable.

'That I'd be a man of straw? Well, you can tell him from me

that I'm not one of those in the sense he probably has in mind.'

'You did use the word "us", though,' said Crosby mildly.

Stuart Bellamy remained unperturbed. 'My boss merely wishes to live there and asked me to undertake some preliminary enquiries on his behalf. Which I accordingly did.'

'I understand your approach was not successful, sir,' said Crosby.

'Too right. It wasn't even welcome. I got a first class brush-off but I don't suppose he told you that.'

'No.'

'Lionel Perry said that Berebury Homes' plans were far too advanced to consider change of direction – or words to that effect.'

'And who,' asked Crosby, 'is your employer?' From Crosby's standpoint any name was better than no name.

'Mr Burke,' said Stuart Bellamy readily enough. 'Mr Jason Burke. I tell you this in confidence. He doesn't want the whole wide world to know that he is in the market to buy the place, though, so we would be very grateful if his interest could be treated as commercially sensitive.'

'I quite understand, sir.' Detective Constable Crosby dutifully took down the name and the address of a house in the far north of Calleshire. It was not in his manor and the name of Jason Burke meant nothing to him. He snapped his notebook shut and got to his feet. 'Thank you, sir, you've been very helpful.'

As he drove back down Acacia Avenue in his unmarked police car, Crosby spotted the approach of a car with a man at the wheel. He waited and watched as it pulled up opposite number eight and the engine killed, while the driver surveyed the house without getting out. After a minute or two the engine was switched on again and the car driven away. Crosby automatically took down its number before driving back to the police station.

CHAPTER ELEVEN

'My name,' Jason Burke's manager spoke slowly and clearly down the telephone, 'is Stuart Bellamy and I would like to talk to the chairman of the Berebury Preservation Society.' Stuart Bellamy had sat in his sitting room for quite a long while before taking any action, Jason's valedictory threat still ringing in his ears and Detective Constable Crosby's visit fresh in his mind. 'I understand your society is very concerned about the future of Tolmie Park.'

Actually it would have been quite difficult to avoid the Society's well-publicised attempts to save the building but he did not say so.

'We certainly are,' Wendy Pullen trilled, happily preparing to deliver her usual lecture on the subject. 'We'd do anything we could to save it – anything legal, that is,' she added hastily, since she didn't know to whom she was speaking.

'And my principal,' said Stuart Bellamy incautiously, 'is prepared to do anything to buy it. Well, almost anything.' That last caveat only applied to him: Jason would probably be prepared to go a great deal further than he, Stuart Bellamy, was. But then it was Jason who not only wanted to own Tolmie Park but who was the one who had the money with which to buy it.

'It wasn't you who stole the painting from the museum, was it?' enquired Wendy Pullen curiously. Since Jonathon Ayling, their very own activist and prime suspect for the burglary had denied doing this, she was at a loss to think of anyone else who might have done.

'No,' he said flatly. 'Our only involvement so far has been with Lionel Perry, the chairman of Berebury Homes...'

Stuart heard a hiss down the line at the mention of the name.

'...and Mr Perry has made it abundantly clear that Berebury Homes aren't prepared to sell Tolmie Park to us or anyone else.' What Stuart Bellamy badly needed to know was where he could go from here and he was distinctly short of ideas.

'I'm not surprised,' said Wendy Pullen heatedly, 'not when you work out what they stand to make from developing the land there. But even then you'd have thought they'd have had their price. Everyone else has.'

'Yes.' This was something that Stuart Bellamy couldn't work out either. Anyone would have thought that taking a cheque and laughing all the way to the bank would have been preferable to working one's socks off building houses that nobody wanted built there. And Lionel Perry hadn't even wanted to talk about taking a cheque. It wasn't clear why this should be but Stuart Bellamy could see that it was the first of the many hurdles he would have to clear before being able to report to Jason Burke that he had secured his schoolboy dream for him.

Wendy Pullen had been thinking about something else. She asked tentatively, 'What do the people you are acting for have in mind to do with Tolmie Park, should they get it?'

'Oh, keep it residential,' said Stuart Bellamy. He could almost hear the seraphic look that came over her face.

'Residential,' she breathed. 'How lovely. Just what we were hoping for – a buyer who cared.'

Stuart Bellamy acknowledged that his principal cared very much. He did not say anything about indulging a childhood ambition. Or the holding of open-air pop concerts in the grounds.

'But, of course, you can't tell me his name,' she said, quite forgetting – feminist that she was – that the name might have been that of a woman.

'I'm afraid not,' said Bellamy regretfully.

'I quite understand about commercial secrecy,' she murmured. 'Very important. It's just that sometimes a good name can swing it with a planning committee.'

'Of course,' murmured Bellamy, suppressing the fact that he didn't think in this case Jason's name would.

'Then,' she said briskly, 'we'll just have to think of some other way of helping you. Leave it to me.'

As everyone knows, there is no such animal as complete secrecy. News that there was another buyer in the market for Tolmie Park had reached the bigwigs at Calleford Construction at a speed that had surprised no one in the world of business. And as everyone also knows, all information about a firm that is being stalked by another is grist to the predator's mill.

'If you ask me,' growled their finance director, 'their Lionel Perry is trying to use the reverse chasse glide ploy.'

'You sound like a dancing master,' said his chairman unhelpfully.

'All right then, a killer bee.'

'I still don't get you,' said the chairman, who had reached his present eminence by exhibiting an obstinate refusal to say he understood anything when he didn't. More difficult still for his subordinates to cope with was his tendency to declare that he didn't understand something when he did. Then he would sit back and listen while some poor unfortunate member of staff spelt out an untenable position.

'A reverse chasse glide,' the finance director began again, 'is where a company wants to acquire another company...'

'A take-over,' interrupted the chairman impatiently.

'An attempted take-over,' said the finance director, who wouldn't have got where he had either if he had allowed himself to be railroaded by the chairman at every turn. 'It's when the company being stalked suddenly acquires another firm or a big liability in order to make itself less attractive to the predator.'

'It happens in the animal world,' offered a younger man, his progress in the firm distinctly hampered by a tendency to take his full annual leave, go home on time and not to work through weekends. He was, instead, a promising naturalist and highly thought of by the binocular brigade.

'But this is someone wanting to buy Berebury Homes out,' pointed out the chairman, ignoring this last comment, 'not someone wanting to make them too big to buy.'

'And,' volunteered the promising naturalist, 'we heard that these new people, whoever they are, didn't want to develop the place like Berebury Homes do.'

'No?' snarled the chairman. 'What else could they do with it?'

'Live in it,' suggested the other man. 'At least, that's what I'd heard they wanted to do,' he added hastily as his chairman's expression changed to one of complete and utter disbelief.

Why Lionel Perry of Berebury Homes would not do business with someone who said he was prepared to buy him out for ready money was something that Detective Inspector Sloan could not fathom either. He was, though, giving the question serious consideration.

'Without any strings attached as far as I can see,' added Sloan, grabbing a mug of coffee.

'For cash, too,' said Crosby, who was of an age to regard cash as opposed to credit with a certain amount of simple wonder.

'And who wasn't even interested in checking out the prospective purchaser's financial credentials, let alone asking him why he wanted it,' pointed out Detective Inspector Sloan. 'You'd have thought it was the first thing any real businessman would have done. Quite apart from anything else, there was always the possibility that he was passing up on a very good deal for the firm.'

He was visited by yet another interesting thought. 'I'm no expert on company law, Crosby, but I have an idea that that action might not be legal in itself seeing as a board's first duty is to its shareholders.'

'Doesn't make sense, does it?' agreed Detective Constable Crosby, who was augmenting his own coffee with a Chelsea bun. He brightened. 'It might have been that he was afraid the buyer wanted the place so that he could get up to no good like that Sir Francis Filligree and his pals. Perhaps that Stuart Bellamy wanted to buy Tolmie Park so that they could turn it into a modern – what did that girl at the museum call it? – Hellfire Club? And the present owners – Berebury Homes, that is – didn't want him to.'

Sloan took another sip of his coffee and said drily, 'Lionel Perry didn't strike me as being quite as public-spirited as that, Crosby.' He wondered if he should try to explain to the detective constable that public-spirited actions could – and often did – cover a multitude of sins but then he decided that this was not the moment for a long lecture on the limits of corporate responsibility and went on, 'There must be a better reason than that although I'm blowed if I can think of one. Not offhand.'

Detective Constable Crosby finished off his bun without suggesting any reason at all why Lionel Perry should not have made further enquiries about what had sounded like a very good offer. And more especially why the chairman of Berebury Homes should not have even considered it appropriate to enquire further into the capacity of the prospective purchaser to pay for Tolmie Park, cash down.

'And why should he – or anyone else for that matter – try to burn the place down, anyway?' asked Sloan, adding this to the already long list of imponderables.

'To get it cheaper?' suggested Crosby. 'Damaged goods, you know – second-hand rose – part worn – that sort of thing?'

Detective Inspector Sloan said that since the prospective purchaser appeared to have all the money in the world a damaged building versus an existing one would seem to be irrelevant – in fact a fire sale might even make buying it a less attractive proposition.

'If he's so rich, then how come we don't know him?' asked Crosby.

'That, if I may say so, Crosby, is as sad a commentary on contemporary society as I have ever heard.'

'Yes, sir.'

Nevertheless, Detective Inspector Sloan decided fairly to himself, the constable had a point. The police usually did know the very rich in their patch, for to be rich and a wrong-doer seemed to be the case far too often these days when old money no longer prevailed as it had once done and making great sums of money legally was a great deal more difficult than in days of yore.

And to be rich and upright was to invite theft and thus be known to the police in quite another way.

He set his coffee cup down and said to Crosby, 'I can't tell you why we don't know him but you told me that nothing came up when you checked Stuart Bellamy out.' That adage about not asking any successful man how he had come by his first million pounds still applied when more and more men became millionaires and even when a million pounds wasn't what it had been when Sloan was a boy.

'Clean as a whistle,' said the detective constable, 'but the funny thing is that although the chap he was acting for is quite a different kettle of fish...'

'Jason Burke?'

'Him. He's as clean as a whistle, too. Even though,' here the constable delivered his punch-line with relish, 'he's the one who uses the stage name of Kevin Cowlick.'

Sloan sat back and allowed himself to relax for a long moment. 'That at least might explain the money. That man's a real pop idol if ever there was one.'

A set-up where one man acted for another; where men used more than one name; where men had more money than they knew what to do with; where they got other people to launder that money for a cut of it; where men – and all too often now, poor women – were metaphorically taking in each other's fiscal washing and returning it actually – legally – squeaky clean, which was the object of the whole exercise; were now all part of today's policing.

'And whether,' Sloan said, 'you happen to consider the man's gains ill-gotten or not I suppose comes down to whether or not you like his music.' There were those folk – his own mother for one – who would not allow it even to be called music.

'Yes, sir,' said Crosby.

'And as to why he or anyone else should want to nick the painting from the museum, I couldn't begin to guess,' said Sloan, mentally adding this fact, too, to his list of all the other unknowns in the case that had surfaced so far. 'Perhaps if this Kevin Cowlick wanted the house that badly and couldn't buy it in the end, his man...'

'Stuart Bellamy?' supplied Crosby.

'Stuart Bellamy could have thought the painting might make a good souvenir.'

Crosby was examining the tips of his fingers with interest, having seemingly forgotten that Chelsea buns were sticky. 'If you ask me, sir, he seemed a bit worried about it all – as if his job was on the line – you know, that sort of thing.'

Sloan rejected this out of hand. 'The painting is a portrait of the fourth baronet – there's not a lot of the house in it.'

'So what could there be in it for Lionel Perry and his crowd in building new houses that's better than selling without doing any work?' asked Crosby, licking his fingers.

'I can see that this line of reasoning would appeal to you, Crosby,' he said. 'What indeed?'

'If you ask me, it would save a lot of effort.'

'It would be much better, too, than the uncertainty of waiting for planning permission,' Sloan reminded him, still convinced that this was a factor in the equation – which particular equation he was less sure about.

'Sure thing,' said Crosby, his diction somewhat impaired by the finger-licking.

'You say that this Jason Burke is young?' said Sloan.

'His sidekick says so,' said Crosby.

'Not that Stuart Bellamy is all that old himself, but he's older than Burke.'

'I think,' said Detective Inspector Sloan, 'that a visit to Jason Burke is called for quite soon.'

Young and rich was not a common combination and it would be interesting to meet someone who was both.

Jonathon Ayling hobbled out of his office in the slippers the police had left him with and stepped into the reception area of Berebury Precision Engineers. 'They've taken my shoes away,' he said to the girl there, pointing to his feet.

'They can't do that,' she said.

'I know they can't,' he snapped.

'Not without arresting you,' she said, worldly wise.

'But what was I supposed to do? Say they couldn't have them and let them draw their own conclusions?'

'I thought you said you hadn't done anything wrong,' she said pertly.

'I haven't and therefore I'd be glad if you'd refrain from telling everyone about the police.'

She stared at him. 'They haven't gone and arrested you, have they?'

'Of course not.'

'Then what were they doing here?'

'Search me,' said Jonathon Ayling.

She giggled. 'They'll do that next time.'

'Don't be like that. Now, I've got some important telephone calls to make so don't let anyone disturb me until I say so.'

'Very well, Mr Ayling,' she said in the mocking tones she imagined were used in upmarket offices.

'Thank you,' he said turning back.

'Thousands wouldn't but I'll keep the mob at bay for you,' she said, waiting until he was out of earshot before ringing her best friend to tell her all about it.

CHAPTER TWELVE

'Only too happy to help you in any way we can, gentlemen.' Lionel Perry took the chair at the head of the boardroom table at Berebury Homes Ltd with the ease of long practice and waved the two policemen into seats opposite. He motioned Auriole Allen to the seat at his side.

'Thank you, sir,' said Detective Inspector Sloan. Having heard this sentiment expressed with varying degrees of sincerity many times before, he immediately dismissed it as worthless. 'For starters we shall be wanting a note of all the movements of you and your staff this morning.'

'I quite understand, Inspector.'

'Especially those of them whose route to work leads past Tolmie Park.'

Perry gave a quick nod. 'Me for a start, Inspector. Actually, I had a puncture not far from there myself this morning – Robert Selby always comes in that way and Derek Hitchin sometimes.' He turned to Auriole Allen. 'You don't, but I don't know about that new fellow…you know, the young one.'

'Ned Phillips,' supplied Auriole Allen. 'He's lodging out beyond Tolmie. In Almstone.'

'Naturally we were all very sorry here to learn about the fire,' Perry went on fluently, 'but I gather from our architect who is over there now that the damage is not irretrievable.'

'That's good,' said Sloan, mentally registering the fact that the chairman of Berebury Homes was not on site now himself, having shown a marked preference for seeing the two policemen on his own home ground.

That home ground obviously included holiday snaps – quite good ones, too – of Swiss mountains. Sloan noted automatically that he was sitting under a fine view of Mont Rosa. It brought back the holiday he and his wife, Margaret, had had in Interlaken. That had been before the advent of their son, which had put foreign holidays out of reach in more senses than one.

Lionel Perry let them have the benefit of one of those benevolent gestures that figured so prominently in his photograph on the front cover of the company's annual report. 'Regrettable as the fire is from our point of view, Inspector, it's more of an inconvenience than a disaster. We had no plans to demolish the house at Tolmie – indeed we shall be looking to our insurers to cover the cost of any reinstatement.'

Detective Inspector Sloan, who had been considering that the fire might have been a positive bonus to the firm, contrived to look interested.

Auriole Allen stirred at Lionel Perry's side. 'Fortunately it had recently been the subject of a full survey.' She picked up a sheet of paper. 'I can let you have a copy of the statement we've just released to the press, Inspector, if that's any help.'

Sloan sat back in his chair as he tried to calculate how many years it had been since he had taken anything in a newspaper at face value, while Crosby perked up and asked

Lionel Perry curiously, 'What's your sort of disaster, then?'

'Any developer could tell you that, young man.' Lionel Perry gave the urbane smile so beloved of his shareholders. 'Great crested newts.'

'Newts?' echoed Crosby in spite of himself.

'Great crested newts. They don't – er – relocate easily. Or – nearly as bad as newts – is having important archaeological remains found on site,' said Perry. 'The regulations say that no development shall take place until the applicant or the developer has secured the implementation of a programme of archaeological work in accordance with a written scheme…how does it go on, Auriole?'

'Written scheme of investigation,' she said, deftly taking up the thread, 'which has been submitted to and approved by the local planning authority.'

Perry sighed. 'So you see, young man, we can always be undone by the Romans.'

'Not refusal of planning permission, then?' put in Sloan before Crosby could complain about being addressed as a young man. It was a sensitive issue with him.

Perry smiled again. 'You can appeal against unreasonable refusal of planning permission, Inspector. There are procedures and guidelines and so forth plus a certain amount of logic…'

Not a lot of it, thought Sloan to himself, if his own experience of bureaucratic life had anything to do with it. Logic was usually thin on the ground.

'…especially if you can cite sustainability,' went on Perry. 'But there's no appeal against newts or a Roman villa.'

'And what's sustainability, then?' asked Crosby.

The chairman of Berebury Homes, Ltd leant back in his chair with the air of a man giving a familiar lecture. 'Sustainability is meeting the needs of the present without compromising the ability of future generations to meet theirs.'

Since Detective Constable Crosby looked quite blank at this, Auriole Allen explained kindly, 'It's achieving the best possible balance between environmental, social and economic issues in the district.'

Crosby's face cleared. 'I get you. What you want but not too much of either.'

'Well put,' said Lionel Perry, metaphorically patting him on the back. 'Anyway, we have no plans to demolish the house. All we want to do is carry out some sympathetic restoration and create a number of attractive living units…'

'Houses and apartments,' translated Auriole Allen swiftly.

'But I understand you haven't got actual permission yet,' advanced Detective Inspector Sloan, putting in his oar. His oar was, after all, the one that counted.

'An application for outline planning permission is with the Berebury Council as we speak,' said Lionel Perry.

'All still in the balance, then,' said Crosby chattily.

'The highways people have raised no objections as far as the traffic situation is concerned,' said the chairman. 'That's most important.'

Detective Constable Crosby's head came up with a jerk at the mention of the word traffic since his main ambition in life was to join F Division's traffic section. This wish was only exceeded by the determination of the traffic section not to have him there.

'The Calleshire County Council has an input, too,' Auriole

Allen obliquely supplemented Lionel Perry like the good employee she was, 'but we understand that they're ready to go along with our plans.'

'And, importantly,' added Perry, 'no neighbours have raised any objections with the planning authority.'

'There aren't any neighbours,' protested Crosby.

'Exactly, constable,' said Perry with the air of a schoolmaster giving a pupil full marks.

Detective Inspector Sloan leafed through the pages of his notebook. 'We are in the process, sir, of investigating some – er – additional material found at the site.'

'Really? What sort of material? Tell me.'

'We wonder if you could throw any light on why there should have been a pile of bones in the middle of the billiard room floor.'

'Bones? Good God! You mean there was a person there when the building went up?' The colour of the man's face went from healthy pink to a deadly ashen.

'Just a pile of bones,' said Sloan.

Lionel Perry looked genuinely stricken. 'As far as we were concerned, Inspector,' he said, recovering himself a little, 'the building had been empty for a couple of years at least. I have absolutely no idea why there should have been anyone there.'

'There wasn't,' said Detective Sloan quietly. 'The bones aren't human.'

Lionel Perry sank back in his chair, patently relieved. 'Thank God for that.'

'What we would also like to know, sir, is why those bones should have been sitting on a pile of lobster shells.'

The change in the man was startling. 'Lobster shells?' he

echoed shakily. His face, which had been starting to resume its usual colour, reverted to an ashen-white.

'Genus Homarus,' said Detective Inspector Sloan, automatically noting that the chairman's hands had now acquired a distinct tremor.

'I've no idea at all,' Lionel Perry said in a voice now grown quite husky.

But, as Detective Inspector Sloan was later to report to Superintendent Leeyes, 'He was lying.'

Derek Hitchin, Berebury Homes's project manager, walked well away from Randolph Mansfield in the grounds of Tolmie Park, fished out his mobile telephone from his pocket and punched in the number of the direct line to the planning officer at Berebury Council.

'That you, Jeremy?' he said.

'It is,' said a voice cautiously.

'Derek here.'

'You don't have to tell me that.'

'Are you alone?'

'As it happens, yes, but remember that it's something you can't always count on.'

'Look here, Jeremy, we're going to have to put in some revised plans for Tolmie Park.'

'Word had reached us,' said Stratton neutrally.

'Not a big amendment.'

'You surprise me.' The planning officer did not sound at all surprised.

'Nothing too significant.'

'I see. Just a little local difficulty, then,' said Stratton ironically.

'Don't be like that. Randolph's bound to be in touch and then take his time over his blasted drawings. Elegant they may be but quick he isn't.'

'I don't know any architects who are,' responded Stratton. 'Occupational disease of the profession.'

'I don't need to tell you, Jeremy, that there's a lot riding on our getting the project started soon,' said Derek Hitchin.

'And I don't need to tell you,' said Stratton, 'that that, of course, is not really the concern of the local authority.'

'There's a very great deal riding on it, actually,' said Hitchin. 'Including my job.'

'Listed building consent always takes time, too,' said Jeremy Stratton obliquely.

'What matters most,' said Hitchin tightly, 'is the planning committee's decision…'

'But Derek…'

'And what matters to the planning committee is the opinion of their chief planning officer. They listen to him, all right. Even I know that.'

'Berebury Council can't speak for English Heritage…and you should know that, too.'

'They're no trouble,' said Hitchin confidently. 'After all, we're saving an old building. Our worry is that the fire is the work of Calleshire Construction – delaying things while they limber up for a takeover.'

'Strictly speaking, that is not the concern of the local authority either.'

'Well, it's certainly ours with bells on. And if it wasn't them who did it then my money's on the Berebury Preservation Society.'

'They are indeed a very active local interest group,' said Jeremy Stratton guardedly.

'Their Jonathon Ayling really gets my goat.'

But Jeremy Stratton was much too much a local government servant to be drawn into comment on that young man over the telephone.

Or on anything else.

It was purely a question of following routine that made Detective Inspector Sloan telephone his opposite number in Calleford. 'We're checking on something over here at Berebury,' he said, 'and we'd like the low-down on an outfit over your way.'

'Fire away.'

'Calleford Construction. It's a building firm.'

'I'll say it is,' said the man warmly. 'The biggest and best in Calleshire – that's according to them, of course.'

'And is it?' said Sloan, who hadn't been born yesterday.

He could hear his opposite number sucking his teeth. 'Biggest, certainly. As for being the best, I wouldn't know. I don't live in one of their houses.' He sniffed. 'Probably the only person round here who doesn't.'

'Like that, is it?' said Sloan.

'If there's room on the land to build a house then Calleshire Construction'll build two there. Or three.'

'Anything known?' enquired Sloan since overcrowded building was only an aesthetic crime.

'No funny business – that's as far as we've heard, of course.'

'Of course.' That was a given in all police work.

A cackle came down the phone line. 'No need for funny

business, anyway. Money running out of their ears. Must be, with this housing boom.'

That, thought Sloan, was a sad reflection on business morality if ever there was one. Although, he reminded himself, on the other hand, the association between crime and pressing need applied to drug-taking clearly enough. He contented himself with saying, 'There's a suggestion this end that Calleshire Construction might be planning a takeover of Berebury Homes.'

'Eat or be eaten,' said the voice from Calleford. 'Law of the jungle.'

No head of a criminal investigation department, however small that department, needed to be told about the law of the jungle. 'So a takeover might be on the cards then?'

'Calleford Construction could probably have them for breakfast.' Food was clearly still in the mind of Sloan's opposite number. 'It would be an obvious move for them. There are the economies of scale for starters...'

'Small is beautiful.' Sloan quoted someone famous. He wasn't sure who. Yes, he was. Schumacher. The superintendent had the sentiment on the calendar in his office as part of his campaign against the amalgamation of police forces.

'And there's something else I've always found big business keen on.'

'Besides money?'

Sloan's irony went unremarked. 'Consolidation,' said the other man.

Sloan roughly translated that into, 'If you can't beat them, join them.'

'So what's your problem over in Berebury, then?' asked his opposite number.

'Arson,' Sloan settled for the one thing that he was sure about. 'Damage to a building due for redevelopment.'

The voice at the other end of the line gave this due consideration before asking, 'Would that be good or bad for your firm?'

Detective Inspector Sloan sighed. 'Part of the trouble is that for the life of me, I don't know. Delay might weaken it – upset the finances and so on – if it holds up development.'

'Calleford Construction would get their hands on it for less then. Delay would hold them up, too, of course…'

'But then, they could afford it,' concluded Sloan. 'Is that what you're saying?'

'On the other hand…'

'Yes?' One of the first things every police officer learnt when appearing in court was that there was invariably an 'other hand'. It was something defence lawyers were always very keen on.

'On the other hand,' said his opposite number, 'arson often facilitates redevelopment.'

'We'd thought about that, too.'

'Heads you win, tails you win,' offered the man in Calleford philosophically. 'I can tell you one thing for nothing,' he went on, 'and that's that the head honcho at the firm over here is one of the smartest cookies around. No flies on him and he doesn't take prisoners, either.'

'I have news for you, Jason,' grinned Stuart Bellamy, pushing open the pop star's studio door. 'The fuzz are after us.'

'It's all up, then is it?' Jason Burke looked up, unalarmed. He was fiddling with a synthesiser in the corner. 'By the way,

Stu, I don't think that's what they call the police any more. It's dated.'

'Right,' conceded Bellamy, bowing to a higher realism. One of the things that performers like Kevin Cowlick had to be was up-to-date in current slang all the time.

Jason pushed a knob up a little, cocked his head to listen to the adjusted sound, and then said, 'What is it we are meant to have been and gone and done, then? Tell me.'

Stuart Bellamy, accountant marque, grinned and said, 'I think it's to have enough money to make an offer for Tolmie Park, cash on the nail.' He frowned. 'At least, I think that's the crime. They're very hot on money-laundering these days.'

'What about those spreadsheet thingies you do each year for the tax people?'

'Balance sheet and income and expenditure account?' Stuart was never sure how much of Jason's professed ignorance was genuine.

'Them. You're the one who's always saying they're so important. Not me, mate.'

'They are,' insisted Bellamy, 'but of course the Berebury Homes people haven't seen them yet.'

Jason Burke moved over to the piano and started to strum his way through a scale. 'Should be good enough for them when they do.'

Stuart Bellamy appreciated that this was the nearest Jason Burke – or Kevin Cowlick for that matter – would come to awarding him an accolade for good management.

Jason cocked his thumb at a shelf full of singles, 'If not, those should be good enough for 'em instead.'

'They should. But don't forget that they don't know about

those yet, either,' Bellamy reminded him, 'but I expect they will pretty soon.' He frowned. 'I've been wondering why the police have got on to us so quickly in the first place. I think it might have been my fault for mentioning readily available funds to Lionel Perry so early on.'

'For which read cash,' said Jason.

'I guess he told the police and they always get twitchy when there's a lot of money around that they don't know about and which hasn't been in somebody's family for yonks.'

Jason's fingers hit the top of the scale with a thump. 'According to the radio, there's not a lot of damage from the fire at Tolmie Park. And all of it confined to the billiard room, which is stuck on the back anyway.'

'That's good,' said Bellamy, trying to sound as if he meant it. Buying Tolmie Park wasn't going to be easy whichever way you looked at it.

'Strikes me as downright fishy,' said Burke frankly. 'You really didn't do it, Stu, did you?'

Bellamy looked at him warily. He still never knew when Burke was joking and when he was being deadly serious. The pop star's calculatedly expressionless face went down well with his fans; his deadpan look made life very difficult for everyone else.

'Cos your job's on the line if you did, Stu. You know that, don't you?'

'Course I didn't, Jason. Arson couldn't have helped you buy the place any way you look at it.'

'It must have been meant to help somebody do something,' said the pop star, wise in his generation.

'Ah, I do think you're right there, Jas. Otherwise the

police wouldn't be noseying around like they are.'

'So you can go straight ahead, then, and open negotiations, can't you?' said Burke. 'What's your next move going to be?'

Bellamy frowned. 'I think we should let Douglas Anderson at the bank know that one of these days we'll be wanting to spend big money all at once. It never does any harm to prepare the ground with your money people.'

'And quite soon, Stu. Tell him that we'll be wanting it quite soon and to have the dibs ready.'

'Point taken,' said Stuart Bellamy, retreating to the cubby-hole that constituted his office without telling Jason that 'dibs' wasn't what they called money these days.

It was Ned Phillips who met Randolph Mansfield and Derek Hitchin when they returned to the offices of Berebury Homes from the damaged Tolmie Park. 'Message from Mr Selby,' he said to the new arrivals. 'He's had to go over to see the bank manager about something. He said to say he wants both your opinions about the damage as soon as possible...'

'Funny, isn't it, that he always wants things quickly when it takes such an age to get any figures out of him,' said Hitchin.

'He wants to know about the damage both from an insurance point of view and from a planning one,' hurried on Ned Phillips.

'And ne'er the twain shall meet,' said Mansfield sourly. 'Nobody understands that there are some things about old buildings that you can't quantify. He thinks an architect is just a builder who's been to a finishing school.'

'The trouble,' grumbled Hitchin, 'is that our Robert also thinks that planning is something that you can quantify. Well, you can't. It's more organic than that. If you ask me, it's more like being in the lap of the gods.'

'It's certainly more luck than judgement,' said Mansfield, ever the architect.

'I thought there were guidelines,' said Ned Phillips tentatively, looking alertly from one man to the other.

'Guidelines not tram lines,' said Hitchin. 'With tram lines at least you know where they're going...'

'And where they end,' put in Mansfield.

'Guidelines,' said Hitchin, 'are what you might call, "always open to interpretation".'

'Bah,' said Mansfield.

'Er – I see,' said Ned Phillips hastily. 'Not helpful but still constraining.'

'Especially when you want to be really innovative,' said the architect. 'Good design should be a living thing.'

'Mind you,' said Derek Hitchin, casting a sly glance at the architect, 'radicalisation can be impractical.'

'Only sometimes,' came back Randolph Mansfield. Turning to Ned Phillips, he said, 'None of this is your headache, anyway. It's mine. Tell Mr Selby I'll let him have his report just as soon as I can.'

'Copy to the chairman,' added Phillips. 'I forgot to say that.'

Hitchin sniffed, 'There always is. Lionel likes to be kept in the picture.'

Mansfield gave a hollow laugh. 'Not that he always understands the principles of good design.'

'Or the difficulties of carrying it out,' said Hitchin, more graciously than was usual for him.

'Right...' said Ned Phillips uncertainly, going on, 'but then I suppose chairmen are meant to be looking at the big picture.'

'True.' Mansfield stroked his chin. 'So they say, anyway. Sometimes they're just minding their backs.'

'Can't always see the wood for the trees, though, some of 'em,' said Hitchin.

'The big picture and the future,' said Mansfield, 'that's what they're meant to be looking at.'

'Ah,' said Hitchin. 'The future. Now, there's a thing.'

Ned Phillips looked from one man to the other. 'What's up with the future?'

Derek Hitchin said, 'Nothing for you to be worrying your pretty little copper-nob about, laddie.'

Ned Phillips flushed.

'Be like us,' said Randolph Mansfield, 'and worry instead about why there was what is euphemistically called "a heavy police presence" at Tolmie Park since the fire. They want to interview us all about where we were this morning when the fire started.'

'Police?' stammered Phillips, his flush fading as quickly as it had come. 'But I thought...' His voice fell away before he had completed the sentence.

'But you thought what?' asked the architect curiously.

'Nothing,' said Phillips. He shook his head. 'Nothing at all.'

CHAPTER THIRTEEN

'That book you sent me to look up, sir,' Detective Constable Crosby was standing by Sloan's desk looking uncomfortable. 'The baronetage.'

'Yes?' Sloan himself was studying a message from forensics about lobster shells and glass in shoes.

'It just said "1 s" all the time except when it said "2 s".'

'An heir and to spare,' said Sloan. There had been no doubt about the lobster shells or the glass.

'Beg pardon, sir?'

'Nothing. Go on.' The lobster shells had been sitting on bones from adult beef cattle.

'That "s" stands for son, sir, and he's always called Francis Edward or Edward Francis which makes it difficult.'

'Ringing the changes,' said Sloan absently, turning over the report from forensics who wanted to know if he needed the cattle further identified.

'At least the eldest sons are,' said Crosby.

Sloan sighed. 'Did you copy it out?'

Detective Constable Crosby struggled with a piece of paper stuck in his pocket. 'That man who went to Switzerland, he died there in the war, leaving a baby son. He grew up and married...'

'Those two stages in life, let me remind you, Crosby, don't always go together these days.'

'No, sir.' Crosby was still a bachelor. 'And that Filligree had two sons and a daughter and they had sons and daughters.'

Sloan said, 'So there are still some of them around?' For a fleeting moment he wondered whether they all had what Thomas Hardy had called 'the family face'. It was his wife who liked Hardy – he hadn't been struck on his writing – not a man's writer, he decided. That was until she had made him listen to the poem:

> *I am the family face;*
> *Flesh perishes, I live on*
> *Projecting trait and trace*
> *Through time to times anon.*

He'd liked that and remembered it as he realised how absurdly pleased he had been at the christening of his own baby son when someone had remarked on the boy's likeness to his grandfather.

'Yes, sir.' Crosby consulted the crumpled piece of paper. 'And it's the turn of the eldest to be Edward Francis.'

Detective Inspector Sloan laid the report from forensics down on his desk. He would decide later whether to ask the clever scientists there if the bones had come from a cow called Daisy or a bull called Taurus. 'Since routine is what makes detection what it is,' he said, 'I suppose we'd better track the latest Filligree down. You can be getting on with that, Crosby. That's after we've taken some statements from the staff at Berebury Homes about their route to work this morning.'

These proved singularly unhelpful. Randolph Mansfield lived at the other side of the county and never came past Tolmie Park. Robert Selby always came to work that way.

'No, Inspector,' he said when interviewed. 'There was certainly no smoke visible when I came by. I do, of course, get in quite early these days. My department is very busy just now and I have to put in a long day just to keep up with the workload.' He shook his head. 'No, I didn't see Lionel at all but then I wouldn't expect to have done. He doesn't usually get in until much later.'

Derek Hitchin said breezily, 'Yes, I came that way. Don't always but I did this morning. No, I didn't see Lionel's car at all but then he would have been later than those of us who have to earn our crust.'

'Quite so,' said Sloan. 'And any sign of fire? Did you see smoke?'

'Nope. I wouldn't have gone any further if I had, would I?'

'I suppose not,' said Sloan, who supposed no such thing. 'By the way, the gate to the drive over there was locked when the fire brigade arrived. Do you know who has keys?'

'Anyone who needs to go over there collects them from the office,' said Hitchin. 'They're on a hook there.'

'Labelled?'

'Course they're labelled, Inspector. Tolmie Park isn't the only development we're working on, you know. Fine mess we'd all be in if we didn't know which key was which.'

Auriole Allen lived between Berebury and Calleford and thus did not pass Tolmie Park. 'And I was a little bit later than usual this morning, Inspector,' she admitted. 'I stopped off on the way to collect the local paper. It's the one I have to keep my eye on most.'

Ned Phillips was willing but uninformative – up to a point, that is. 'Yes, I came in that way from Almstone first thing but I didn't see anything out of the ordinary. Mind you, Inspector, you need to keep your eyes on the road that way. Before you know where you are there'll be a tractor in front of you and no room to pass. Anyway the house is too far from the road to see it properly.'

Sloan asked whether he had seen Lionel Perry's car on the road.

'The Jag? No, but I took it round to the garage for them to mend the spare after he'd had a flat. The garage couldn't find a puncture. They said it was a loose valve.'

Detective Inspector Sloan made yet another note in his records.

'I can only report the establishment of some facts, sir,' said Detective Inspector Sloan. 'Nothing more.' Duty bound, he was keeping in touch with Superintendent Leeyes.

'About some definite offences, though, I take it?' said Leeyes pertinently. 'Police time is valuable.'

'A portrait has been taken from the museum and there has been arson at Tolmie Park. More than that, sir, I can't say. Not at this stage.'

Leeyes grunted.

'But there are certainly some other matters, sir, that require further investigation and may have some bearing on the situation – such as the burnt bones.'

'There's no need to speak like a rookie giving evidence, Sloan. You're not in court now.'

'No, sir.' He took a deep breath. 'For starters, someone broke a window at the museum and entered without activating the alarm system...'

'And got out again, presumably,' said Leeyes.

'Unless it was an inside job, the alarm might well have been silenced by an expert and Jonathon Ayling...'

'He of the Nimby Brigade?'

'Beg pardon, sir?'

'Not In My Backyard. Nimby. The "build what you like but not near me" crowd. Got it?'

'Yes, sir.' Sloan didn't like acronyms. 'Him, although Tolmie Park isn't very near anyone. The firm that Jonathon Ayling works for installs burglar-alarms. Crosby's gone back to the museum to see if Berebury Precision Engineering put theirs in for them and then he's going out to tell Ayling that we want to interview him.'

Leeyes grunted again.

Sloan forged on. 'I think the theft of the portrait of Sir Francis Filligree is where the puzzle begins.' He coughed. 'We have been trying to establish the present whereabouts of the current baronet but without success so far.'

'Ah,' said the superintendent alertly. 'So there's one about.'

'Somewhere, I think,' said Sloan. 'But where I couldn't say. Another complication is the fact that a young man called Jason Burke had apparently expressed an interest in buying the Tolmie Park estate.'

'Just like that?' asked the superintendent.

'Outright. Without strings. Lionel Perry of Berebury Homes

turned him down flat without giving him the option of making him an offer.'

'Thought he was having him on, I expect,' said the superintendent.

'But we don't know how Burke took that.'

'Ah,' said Leeyes alertly, 'so this Burke sets it on fire, taking the view that if he couldn't have it, then he would see that nobody else could either?'

Sloan searched for the right words, taking care not to imply that his superior officer could be jumping to conclusions. 'I don't think that we can go as far as that just yet, sir.'

'This Jason Burke,' said Leeyes thoughtfully. 'How was he going to pay for Tolmie Park? Do we know that? He wouldn't get it for peanuts, not unless the developers didn't get their planning permission.' He looked up and said sharply, 'Sloan, we haven't stumbled on some money-laundering, have we?'

'I don't think so,' said Sloan. The superintendent was inclined to use the royal 'we' when there was any prospect of a really successful case being solved. 'You see, Jason Burke is the real name of Kevin Cowlick.'

Leeyes sat up. 'What, that nerd with the long hair who gives those ghastly musical performances?' Pop concerts ranked high on the list of unhappy interactions between police and public.

'Him,' said Sloan succinctly.

'Then, if he's not money-laundering, he must have got his money from drugs,' concluded Leeyes, a thoroughly modern Peeler.

Detective Inspector Sloan shook his head. 'No. I've been on to our drugs section and they say that although they always pick up a few users at his concerts, he's stayed clean.'

Leeyes grunted. 'Makes a change.'

Sloan studied the papers on the desk. 'I understand we have to thank his doctor for that.'

'How come?'

'Frightened him with a needle when he was young. Apparently this young Jason still runs a mile at the sight of a hypodermic syringe.'

Leeyes grunted again.

'And our man at headquarters who knows about these things tells that Burke could have made the money to buy Tolmie Park or anywhere else you care to name with the proceeds of his albums. Easily.'

Superintendent Leeyes said something indistinguishable about policemen who earned their pittance with hard work.

'There's something else, sir.' Sloan thought it better to hurry on. 'It would also be helpful to know why Lionel Perry was so upset to learn about the bones and the lobster shells. Those really shook him.'

'Someone,' observed Leeyes profoundly, 'is playing funny games.'

'But who with, sir? That's what I would like to know. With us? Or with someone else?'

'Well, find out, Sloan, and soon. There's that money thing you're supposed to be working on.'

'Transactional fraud.'

'That's it. Well, it's important to be getting on with that, too.'

It was something he didn't need telling.

* * *

Wendy Pullman of the Berebury Preservation Society was telephoning someone else. It was Jonathon Ayling at Berebury Precision Engineers this time.

'Wendy,' he protested, 'you know I don't like being rung up when I'm at work.'

She brushed this aside. 'I've heard, Jonathon, that you've had a visit from the police and I want to know if it's true.'

'My middle names are George Washington and I cannot tell a lie.'

'Let's have the truth, then,' she said.

'If you really want to know the sordid details an Inspector called – oh, and he had a constable with him who looked as if running late was the only exercise he had.'

'Of course I want to know the details,' she exploded in exasperation. 'What have you done now?'

'*Moi?*' said Jonathon Ayling in his best French.

'*Vous,*' she retorted firmly.

'I am innocent,' he said in mock histrionic tones.

'And what exactly does that mean?'

'That I wouldn't do anything to bring disgrace on the Berebury Preservation Society.'

'I should hope not.'

'Nothing, that is,' he added, fingers crossed, 'where the end doesn't justify the means.'

'That,' she countered, 'is not an argument.'

'I didn't say it was. It's a statement.'

'So what did you do to make the police visit you?'

'They didn't say.'

'Jonathon, I am not prepared to listen to this nonsense any longer.'

'If you must know they wanted to look at my shoes.'

'Your shoes?'

'My footwear, then.'

'So where had you been that they wanted to check?'

'They didn't say that either. Now, Wendy, I must get back to work…'

Her voice took on a more serious note. 'There is a rumour going around that some bones were found after the fire and we're all a bit worried about it.'

He responded with an unusual earnestness. 'If it will reassure everyone, I can truthfully say that I didn't have anything to do with the fire at Tolmie.'

'So what have you been up to, then?' she asked, only half-convinced by what he had said.

'Helping save Tolmie Park – well, some of it, anyway – for posterity. That's what you want, isn't it?'

After he had put the telephone down he added to himself, 'And let us hope that the end justifies the means.'

CHAPTER FOURTEEN

Everyone who works obviously has to do it somewhere, be it at an office desk, a computer workstation, a supermarket check-out, a factory bench, or even down on the farm still. Policemen had places of work, too, but those places weren't often similar to those of other wage-earners. A session with an informant in a seedy downtown café was far removed from a plush office with a receptionist so superior that she has to be convinced that the front door – rather than the tradesman's entrance – was the right one for an officer of the Crown, but Detective Inspector Sloan had worked in both settings.

The bedroom of a startled drug-dealer apprehended in the middle of the night had very little to be said for it as a place of work either but if that was where the work was, then that was where the policeman went. The same went for the bridge over the river at Berebury on whose parapet Detective Inspector Sloan had once spent half a day talking a man out of jumping into the waters below, whilst some of the places in which he had arrested young tearaways were definitely best forgotten.

So when he and Crosby reached the place of work of Jason Burke and were admitted by Stuart Bellamy, he was able to look round with the detached interest of an impartial observer. Crosby, on the other hand, seemed to be under the impression that he was entering the holy of holies. 'So this is where Kevin Cowlick hangs out,' he breathed as they entered the studio.

'This is where Jason Burke hangs out,' said Sloan more mundanely, unwilling to describe what the pop star did as work. He looked round at a vast collection of tapes, compact discs and even the odd, old 78 rpm shellac record, but it was the enormous synthesiser against the further wall that had immediately caught Crosby's eye.

'Man, will you take a look at that...' he was saying as the door opened and the pop star came in, or rather, made an entrance.

'Hi,' said Jason Burke, advancing on them with Stuart Bellamy trailing along behind him. The pop star was small and wiry, with an air of purpose that helped explain his rise to the top of the performing pyramid. 'You guys wanting somethin', then?' he asked.

'Just a bit of information,' said Sloan in neutral tones.

The pop star turned to his manager and grinned. 'That's what they always say, isn't it, Stu?'

'I wouldn't know about that,' said Bellamy calmly, adding, 'and I wouldn't have thought you would either, Jason.'

Jason smiled disarmingly and said, 'Stuart here keeps everything in order, including me.'

'I'm glad to hear it, sir,' said Sloan heartily. 'It's a wicked enough world as it is.'

Jason Burke stared at him for a full minute and then went over to a microphone and repeated the words into it, savouring them as he did so. 'Sorry about that, but they might make a good start to a lyric.' He began to hum the words, 'It's a wicked enough world as it is,' under his breath. When they were duly recorded he flipped the fringe of hair known as a cowlick away from his forehead and said, 'Now what was it exactly that you wanted to know?'

Without waiting for an answer, he went on to leave them in no doubt about what it was that he himself wanted. 'Tolmie Park, Inspector. I've always wanted it and I have every intention of having it.' He fixed Sloan with a beady eye and said, 'And I don't care what I have to pay to get it. Do you get me there?'

'Receiving you loud and clear,' said Crosby unexpectedly.

Detective Inspector Sloan was more concerned about whether or not what Jason Burke was prepared to do to get hold of Tolmie Park was legal but this didn't seem the right moment to say so. 'Why didn't you buy it before Berebury Homes did, then?' he asked him, ignoring Crosby's intervention.

'Because, Inspector, I didn't know it was up for sale then, that's why. Sneaky is what I call the way that it came on the market. Must have been a word in someone's ear.' Jason Burke suddenly looked quite fierce. 'I tell you, if I don't get Tolmie Park in the end I'm going to have it out with the bank man. And if he's been two-timing me, then I'll take my account somewhere else.'

'I see,' said Sloan, considerably entertained by the vision of the young guitarist reprimanding the portly Douglas Anderson, the middle-aged manager of the Calleshire and Counties Bank. It told him more than anything else about the state of the pop star's wealth – and when he came to think about it, it told him a great deal about the changing values in a changing world. If Jason Burke had ever once walked into the manager's office as a supplicant, he certainly didn't do so any longer.

'And I'll tell him what he can do with his marble and mahogany,' added Jason Burke.

'Tolmie Park…' began Sloan.

'And when you lot find out who set it on fire – if you ever do – then I'm going to have something to say to him as well.'

'Or her,' put in Crosby, fresh from a recent lecture on equal opportunities.

Jason Burke turned his attention to the detective constable. 'You're right there, mate. Mustn't forget the ladies.'

Stuart Bellamy coughed. 'We have registered with the bank that Jason here is interested in buying the property should anything fall through with the financing of the development by Berebury Homes.'

'Interested!' snorted Jason Burke. 'I'm more than interested. I'm going to have that place if it's the last thing I do.'

'I meant should Berebury Homes not get all the planning permissions and so forth that they want,' went on his manager smoothly, 'it is not impossible that it might come back on the market.'

'Not get nothing,' interrupted Jason Burke. 'I want it and I mean to have it. You do understand that, Inspector, don't you?'

Detective Inspector Sloan understood a number of things. The one that mattered most was that Jason Burke might well be carefully making his feelings so widely known that no one was likely to take any of his involvement with Tolmie Park as other than an innocent wish to fulfil a childhood ambition.

And of one thing Sloan was quite sure and that was that Jason Burke was not naïve. One thing that could be said for a backstreet upbringing was that a youth matured early.

'So I told Stu here,' the pop star said, 'to get our legal eagles to start to look into their side of things. It'll save time in the long run.'

In Detective Inspector Sloan's considerable experience getting involved with lawyers never accelerated anything, but he was going to let this young man find that out for himself.

Wendy Pullen, a born conspirator, rang Stuart Bellamy back quite quickly. 'I've come back to you with a plan,' she said, 'which I'd like to run past you.' She was ringing him on his mobile phone and still didn't know who the man was acting for but she was not going to let a little thing like that deter her from doing anything that might help save Tolmie Park – or indeed stop her from taking action right now. 'I'll need your help, though.'

'Go on,' said Stuart Bellamy warily.

'What I think we – that is, I – should do is to issue a press release to let the whole world know that there is a working possibility that Tolmie Park might be reverting to single occupancy.'

Bellamy considered the idea, well aware that Joe Public was a fickle friend at the best of times – and also at best a potentially dangerous one. A press release could turn out to be the loosest of loose cannons.

'That way,' she went on before he could speak, 'the planning people will be made aware that there is another option besides letting the land go for housing – that of a single owner.'

'True.' Bellamy tried to sound enthusiastic. 'Not only all the council, of course, but everyone in Berebury.'

'Exactly,' she said triumphantly. 'The developer's argument for getting enabling permission would be dead in the water once everyone knew that there was something else that could be done with the house and land.'

'Public opinion should be on our side, all right,' he admitted.

'Actually, you never can tell with public opinion,' she said honestly. 'Believe it or not, there were people out there who didn't think the windmill over at Larking worth saving.'

'Never,' said Stuart Bellamy, who was actually still wondering if Berebury Homes would be more likely to sell to Jason if they thought they wouldn't get their enabling permission. His brusque rejection by Lionel Perry at his first approach hadn't been at all encouraging, but, should the council turn Berebury Homes down, a fresh appeal to sell might make a difference.

'Now,' said Wendy, all businesslike, 'what I need to know is how much I can say about this man who wants to buy Tolmie Park and restore it to live in without giving too much about him away.'

'He's a very successful native of the county,' said Bellamy, choosing his words with care, 'having been born and bred in Calleshire.' He was deliberately unspecific about this. Luston was the industrial part of the county that no one ever boasted of coming from. 'But he is now very well known internationally.'

'Perfect,' she said. 'Any family?'

'Not yet,' said Bellamy.' He's still quite young.'

'Better still,' said Wendy Pullen briskly. 'That usually means parties.'

'It does, indeed,' said Bellamy careful not to describe the sort of parties that Jason Burke liked to give.

'And that means work for local people, too,' she went on happily, 'unless that is,' she added suspiciously, struck by a sudden thought, 'he's one of those millionaires who has everything sent down from classy London places.'

'No, no, I'm sure not,' Bellamy hastened to reassure her. 'Don't forget he's a Calleshire boy, born and bred.'

'That'll be my heading,' she said delightedly, 'I'll get onto it straightaway.'

Manners might make the man but in the view of Detective Inspector Sloan it was clothes that made the woman. Or, rather, gave an indication of her cast of mind. In his experience backroom women in cardigans were always the ones with the brains. Naturally, this was no reflection on his wife Margaret, whom he particularly liked to see in a certain mid-blue soft wool dress that went so well with her eyes...

He pulled himself together and pushed further open the glass front door of Arms and the Man, a genealogical research firm in Luston. At first sight the industrial town of Luston seemed a strange place for ancestor-worship but on second thoughts it didn't. Self-made men often wanted to know about their roots – when they could afford the time and the money, that is.

The woman there in the cardigan looked up from her desk

as the two policemen went in. She was surrounded by the largest tomes Sloan had ever seen.

'We're trying to find out about a baronet,' he said, introducing himself.

'That shouldn't be too difficult, Inspector. The armigerous are usually fairly easy to find.'

'The armigerous?' Sloan was too old and too experienced to pretend he knew something when he didn't. It wasted time.

'It means they're entitled to a coat of arms,' she said. 'It's the poor old ag labs that sometimes can be hard to trace.'

'Ag labs?' he queried again.

'Agricultural labourers,' said the genealogist. 'Families forget that when it came to the census most people were servants of the plough.'

'Quite so.' Detective Inspector Sloan, who saw himself as a servant of the Crown, expected that one day his son would be asking about his – and his father's – roots. He must look into it sometime.

Not now.

'So who was it you were looking for?' asked the woman in the cardigan.

'Sir Edward Francis Filligree. The eleventh baronet.'

The head of the woman in the cardigan came up. 'Ah, yes. The Filligrees of Tolmie. A rather uncommon shield. Lobsters couchant, as I remember and...'

'We know about the lobster shells,' said Sloan. 'In the heraldic sense, that is.' What the police didn't know was why they should have been laid out on the billiard room floor at Tolmie Park under a pile of butcher's bones, but this information was not for this woman.

'The Filligrees have owned valuable lobster fishing rights at Edsway over by Kinnisport from way back,' she said. 'That's how the lobsters came to be on their coat of arms.'

For one glorious moment Sloan allowed himself the private luxury of considering what he, Christopher Dennis Sloan, would have on his shield in the unlikely event of his ever being awarded one. Truncheons rampant? Crossed warrants? Magnifying glasses couchant...

'And why their motto is *"le monde est notre homard"*,' she said.

'Come again,' said Crosby.

She turned to him. 'Roughly translated, constable, it means, "The world is our lobster".'

Sloan decided that 'Plod on' would do for his motto. Short and sweet.

'What is really uncommon about the Filligree shield is that it carries the Escutcheon of Pretence,' went on the woman in the cardigan. 'Most interesting.'

The detective inspector, a man who in his time had come across cases of pretence in plenty, had not known that they could reach a man's coat of arms and said so. 'What had the Filligrees been up to, then?' he asked.

'Marrying money,' she said austerely. 'In the eighteenth century.'

'Not a crime.' Money, he thought, might well explain the later improvements to the house and the landscaping.

'Not a crime,' she agreed, 'then or now but essential in the case of some impoverished families.'

Sloan supposed that working in family history brought about a realism all of its own.

'The vicissitudes of families,' she said, demonstrating this, 'usually involve money or sex and when a man marries an heiress...'

'Which is both money and sex,' put in Crosby, his attention fully engaged at last.

'Then this can show on his shield,' she said.

There were feminists whom Sloan knew who would agree with this as only right. Divorce settlements were something else.

'Fancy that,' said Crosby.

'It's a small shield,' explained the genealogist, 'containing the arms of the heraldic heiress which is placed in the centre of her husband's arms in their marital achievements.'

'What are marital achievements?' asked Detective Constable Crosby.

'Do carry on, madam,' said Sloan swiftly.

'Marrying an heiress, of course,' she said, 'can be quite dangerous to the family line.'

'Dangerous?' said Detective Inspector Sloan before Crosby could ask about this, too. He himself had met – and faced, which wasn't the same thing – danger in many forms. Marrying an heiress wasn't one that sprang easily to mind.

'Heiresses come from families with low fertility,' said the genealogist.

'Stands to reason, doesn't it?' said Detective Constable Crosby unexpectedly.

'Quite so,' said Sloan. 'Forgive me, madam, but you seem pretty clued up about the Filligrees of Tolmie.'

'It's rather strange that you should ask about them now, Inspector. Or perhaps it isn't,' she said intelligently. 'Someone else wanted to know, too. About a month or so ago it must have been.'

'Who?' asked Sloan, while Crosby stirred at his side.

'I've got my notes somewhere.' She made a move towards a stack of files. 'Ah, here it is...'

'Name?' persisted Sloan.

'The name he gave,' she said carefully, 'was Smith.'

'Surprise, surprise,' muttered Crosby.

'Address?' said Sloan.

She shook her head. 'He didn't leave an address.'

'Or telephone number?' asked Sloan.

'No, he didn't leave that either. I checked after he'd rung and found that the number had been withheld.' She made a moue of her lips. 'We always do this. I'm sorry to say that people sometimes try not to pay for the research we've done – especially when they find that they're not the long-lost child of a duke after all but someone much lower down the social scale.'

'Or the wrong side of the blanket?' suggested the detective constable helpfully.

'Not necessarily,' she said, 'but in that case they often call it baseborn,' she said. 'Or the bar sinister if you're further up the totem pole.' She turned to Crosby. 'Among the nobility that means illegitimate. It shows as a line down the left hand side of the family tree.'

'This Mr Smith...' said Sloan with commendable attention to the matter in hand, although he was tempted to add something about the Devil always entering stage left.

'He just said he'd ring back,' she said.

'And did he?' asked Sloan.

'Oh, yes,' said the competent woman in the cardigan, consulting her file. 'I made a note that we couldn't trace the current holder of the title for him and told him so when he rang.' She closed the file. 'I'm very sorry that we can't help you either, gentlemen.'

'Were you able to tell anything about him from his voice?' Sloan wanted to know.

'No, Inspector. I think I would have remembered if I had.'

Sloan thought she would, too. He coughed and asked delicately what had happened in the way of payment.

'He asked our charges and the money was in our letterbox the next morning.'

'In cash?' said Sloan.

'In cash,' said the woman in the cardigan.

'Is that Detective Inspector Sloan?' The voice was stilted, formal even. 'My name is Stratton, Jeremy Stratton, and I am the planning officer of Berebury Council. I am telephoning you on the advice of the council's legal department.' The man paused and then went on at something of a rush. 'To report an attempt at bribery and corruption in connection with Tolmie Park.'

CHAPTER FIFTEEN

'Jeremy Stratton, did you say?' Detective Inspector Sloan turned over yet another new page in his notebook and wrote the name down. He was in the council offices in Berebury High Street.

'That's right. I'm the planning officer at Berebury Council.'

'Go on,' said Sloan, mentally adding the crime of attempted bribery and corruption at Tolmie Park to those he already knew about. It was one of the few crimes still in the book where the attempt as well as the achievement of the offence constituted a crime.

'I have received a thinly veiled offer of financial reward over a planning matter in connection with the proposed development out there.' Stratton sat straight up in his chair, oozing rectitude.

'Tell me.'

'An unusual one,' said Jeremy Stratton.

'In what way unusual?' Sloan was beginning to feel that he could no longer be surprised by anything about Tolmie Park.

'It's usually someone wanting their applications granted when they weren't going to be or fast-tracked if they were.'

'An assisted passage, so to speak?' suggested the policeman delicately.

'That is so. This one,' said Jeremy Stratton, 'was indicating that if I was prepared to advise my committee to delay a planning decision out there, there would be something in it for me.'

'Delay?' echoed Sloan, surprised.

'Exactly. That's what's so unusual.' His voice stiffened again. 'I am, in any case, not for sale.'

'Quite,' said Sloan absently. 'And would you have any idea at all of who might benefit by delay in this instance?'

'Pressure groups usually find time helps them raise funds and drum up opposition,' said Stratton astringently.

'I can see that it would,' conceded Detective Inspector Sloan. They had an equivocal view about time and crime down at the police station: sometimes the way ahead became clearer as time went by, sometimes a speedy resolution shocked the guilty into an admission of guilt.

And then there were the cold cases, which were something else.

'Time is what ginger groups usually need most to raise public awareness,' said the planning officer. 'And, if they can afford it, getting on with briefing counsel and so forth.' He tightened his lips and said rigidly, 'They might feel that palm oil might help their cause, but let me tell you, Inspector, that it wouldn't.'

'Tell me, this approach – when did it come – before or after the fire?'

'Before,' said Jeremy Stratton. 'About three weeks ago, actually.'

'Did you report it?'

'Only to our chief executive.'

'How did it come?' asked Detective Inspector Sloan with gritted teeth: far too many people thought involving the police more trouble than it was worth, which was sometimes a pity.

'By telephone to my office. A muffled voice that I didn't recognise.'

'Why tell us this now?' asked Sloan.

'Because I've just had another approach – well, threat, actually.'

'Threat?'

'That I would be accused of misfeasance in public office if I didn't agree to delay matters.'

'Carrying out a legal act illegally?'

'Exactly,' said Stratton. 'The man said it was common knowledge that I was a damn sight too friendly with the project officer at Berebury Homes – a man called Derek Hitchin.'

'But you're just good friends?' said Detective Inspector Sloan without any inflexion at all.

'Planning officers can't afford to have friends,' said Jeremy Stratton bitterly. He added even more bitterly, 'They do have relations, though.'

'Cousin?' suggested Sloan.

'Worse,' said Stratton. 'Brother-in-law. Derek Hitchin.'

'Is there anyone else besides a ginger group you can think of who might benefit from delaying a decision at Tolmie Park?' Sloan asked, making a note.

Stratton paused before saying, 'Theoretically, I suppose a firm's creditors – their suppliers in the ordinary way – if they have them – might prefer new work not to be embarked upon until they were paid for the old.'

Detective Inspector Sloan, family man and salaried, conscious as always of his mortgage, was glad he didn't have any other creditors. The finances of the Sloan household were firmly based on the economic philosophy of Mr Wilkins Micawber.

'On the other hand,' went on the planning officer, 'the creditors might want an early profit to be made so that they could be paid. I wouldn't know about that. Not my pigeon.'

Sloan made a note to check on the finances of Berebury Homes Ltd. It was something he should have done before. 'Anyone else you can think of?'

There was a lengthy pause before Stratton said, 'Strictly speaking it's not my business but I did hear on the grapevine that Calleshire Construction is considering a takeover of the firm.'

Sloan took considerable comfort from the fact that the only outfit that could take over from the police in a democracy were the armed forces of the Crown and that only after the introduction of martial law.

The offer of palm oil, however, was not unknown to the Constabulary either.

'Presumably,' Sloan advanced with a certain diffidence, 'your advice to the appropriate planning committee will be based on the application fulfilling certain criteria?'

'I'll say,' said Jeremy Stratton vigorously. 'It's called a PPG3 and includes the Rural Exemption Plan.'

'Quite,' said Sloan. Statute law was codified, too.

Up to a point.

'As amended, of course,' said Stratton.

'Of course,' said Sloan. Magna Carta and the Breach of the Peace Act had both been amended now. Not that anyone was the better for that.

'Planning Policy Guidance Notes, which is what they are. They're guidance from central government to local planning authorities.'

Detective Inspector Sloan didn't know whether this was good or bad. In the police force you were on your own except for *Stone's Justices' Manual*...

'They're not mandatory, though,' said Stratton. 'Just material considerations.'

The actions in the police force that were mandatory were too numerous to remember, let alone enact.

'And if,' said Sloan, 'someone merely wanted to live there?'

'Nobody could stop them,' said Jeremy Stratton immediately, 'even though we're asked to plan to meet the housing requirements of the whole community, including those in need of affordable and special needs housing.'

'And would the housing development planned for Tolmie Park match that?' The affordability of the Sloan mortgage tended to vary with the seasons, after Christmas being a particularly bad time.

'That would depend on the density of the housing,' said Jeremy Stratton.

'Ah,' said Sloan.

'Naturally Berebury Homes will want to make as much money out of the site as it can.' He sniffed. 'And my guess is that Calleford Construction, if they achieved their takeover, would try to get even more. It's the way they work.'

The way that Detective Inspector Sloan worked was something he was not prepared to discuss with Jeremy Stratton or anyone else.

Save Superintendent Leeyes, that is.

Jonathon Ayling was on the phone. 'Listen, the police have been back again. I've just had that detective constable here. What? No, he hasn't brought my shoes back. He just wants to warn me that I'm to be interviewed about the shards of glass in them matching those from a window that they have concerns about. Why can't they say what they mean and accuse me outright?'

The telephone line crackled.

'Of course I know the answer to that but I wasn't going to tell him, was I? He would only say that the police were pursuing their enquiries.' Ayling removed the receiver from his ear and stared at it. 'Of course, I know it's trite but true,' he said when he put the instrument back to his ear.

'What? They've been on to you, too? Whatever for? You haven't done anything. Oh, just for going past Tolmie. Then you haven't got anything to worry about, have you? Not like me.'

The telephone crackled again.

'Safe? Of course it's safe. Rest assured that Sir Francis Filligree is being properly looked after and as far as I'm concerned you can have him back as soon as it's safe for us to meet and good riddance.'

He paused while the person at the other end of the line spoke. Then he said, 'And if that isn't trouble enough I've had Wendy Pullman on the blower wanting to know exactly what I'm planning for Tolmie Park. For two pins I'd tell her and serve her right. Oh, all right then. I won't.'

His face split into a grin as he cut the connection.

Lionel Perry looked round at his senior staff assembled in the boardroom of Berebury Homes, tapped the table with his pencil, cleared his throat and began. 'I think we can honestly say we're in uncharted waters today...'

'Oh Lord, it's one of his captain-on-the-bridge days,' hissed Derek Hitchin to Robert Selby in an undertone.

'...but nevertheless there are some things that need to be done.' Perry looked down at his notes. 'Auriole is already taking care of the press – that's right, isn't it?'

'If by taking care of, Lionel, you mean that I am giving the *Berebury Gazette* a carefully worded statement disclaiming any responsibility on the part of this firm for the fire at Tolmie Park or for the lobster shells there, then I...'

'Lobster shells?' Derek Hitchin gave a little snort. 'First I've heard of them.'

This was not surprising since Lionel had not seen fit to mention the lobster shells to anyone except Auriole Allen and to nobody at all about the bones.

Randolph Mansfield leant forward. 'Surely lobsters are the Filligree trademark? The one on their coat-of-arms. It's on the top of all the rainwater heads that have survived, too.'

'The hopper-heads,' put in Derek Hitchin.

'So I understand,' said the chairman shortly.

'So why should there be real lobster shells there at Tolmie

Park now?' asked the architect. 'The place doesn't belong to the Filligrees any more. I don't suppose the lobster beds do either.'

Robert Selby, the financial controller, pushed his own papers forward on the table. 'Does it matter?' he said irritably, 'when there's so much to be done now?'

Mansfield subsided back in his seat. 'Perhaps not but...'

Auriole Allen resumed the lead and forged on. 'So in that respect only – issuing a statement – could I be said to be taking care of the press in the sense you mean.' She looked round at them. 'You do realise all of you, don't you, that nobody, but nobody, can stop them printing anything the Berebury Conservation Society choose to tell them about Tolmie Park?'

Derek Hitchin said, 'I'd like to tell them what I think about Jonathon Ayling and his precious Preservation Society but I don't suppose they'd publish that.'

Auriole Allen said, 'And I also told them that we can't throw any light either on the theft of the portrait of Sir Francis Filligree that they told me about because Berebury Homes has never had any connection with the Filligrees.'

'I heard,' said Hitchin slyly, 'that the police have already questioned someone about that – the Preservation Society's precious Jonathon Ayling.'

'The press were a bit guarded about that,' said Auriole Allen. 'They aren't going to print anything yet on that front.'

'Thank you, Auriole.' Lionel Perry tapped his pencil on the table to get their attention. 'Robert here,' he pointed to the financial controller, 'is getting on with setting up an insurance claim.'

'It's under way,' said Robert Selby, barely lifting his head from his papers.

'And,' went on Lionel Perry, consulting his notes again, 'Randolph here will no doubt let us know what, if anything, needs doing on the architectural front.'

Randolph Mansfield nodded and then seemed to retreat into a brown study.

'And who is seeing off Calleford Construction?' demanded Derek Hitchin truculently. 'That's what I want to know.'

There was an uneasy pause, then Lionel Perry said lightly, 'Derek, I know you are a man of infinite resource but I hope we are all united in how we deal with Calleford Construction, which is to carry on working exactly as usual. That is what we have been advised is the best policy in the circumstances.'

'I should warn you that their great white chief is a hard man,' said Derek Hitchin, with the clear implication that the chairman of Berebury Homes wasn't.

Auriole Allen rose to Lionel Perry's defence. 'In the business world, Derek,' she said, a hint of reproof in her voice, 'the opposite of a hard man is a fair one.'

'In my vocabulary, Auriole, the opposite of hard is soft,' responded Hitchin.

There was nothing soft in what Lionel Perry started to say next. His voice underwent a sea-change and developed quite a different tone. It suddenly became very cold and steely. 'I repeat that I hope we are all united in how we deal with the threat from Calleford Construction.' He looked round the room. 'Well, aren't we?'

'Of course we are, Lionel,' began Auriole Allen. 'After all, we've all got a lot to lose if Berebury Homes is taken over.'

'All of us,' repeated Lionel Perry softly. 'I think.'

'Our jobs for starters,' said Derek Hitchin. 'Probably.' Privately, he thought Calleford Construction would take him – but not everybody – on their pay-roll any day.

'That's what I said,' murmured Auriole Allen, puzzled. 'Calleford Construction would swallow us whole once they got their hands on us. They're really big.'

'They wouldn't even hiccup,' said Derek Hitchin. 'One gulp would do.'

'That's right, Robert, isn't it?' said Lionel Perry, staring at the financial controller.

Robert Selby nodded without speaking.

'Which is why it's important that we have this plan of normal working and stick to it,' said Lionel Perry.

'Sure,' said Hitchin. 'Stands to reason.'

But Lionel Perry wasn't looking at Hitchin. His gaze was still on Robert Selby.

'So why, Robert,' he said icily, 'were you talking to Calleford Construction's director of finance in the bank today?'

'Me?' Selby flushed. 'For God's sake, Lionel, I wasn't doing anything more than passing the time of day with the man. We were both in the same waiting room, that's all, with appointments to see the manager.' His voice took on a high, strangled note. 'What on earth are you implying?'

He didn't get an answer.

CHAPTER SIXTEEN

Auriole Allen cried 'Oh, Randolph, it was just like that terrible scene in Shakespeare's "King Richard III", do you remember, when the king suddenly turns on Lord Hastings and accuses him of treachery?' They were both standing in the corridor outside the boardroom, not a little shocked.

Lionel Perry had stormed out of the boardroom and then out of the building to his car. They heard a throaty roar as it sped away.

She shivered, 'It was just after the Bishop of Ely had sent to Holborn for strawberries.'

Randolph Mansfield nodded. 'And while we're talking executions, don't forget that Lord Hastings wasn't the only one to end up in the Tower.'

Auriole Allen said shakily 'Who else?'

'The Duke of Buckingham,' said Randolph Mansfield.

'I meant who else of us.'

'Why Robert of all people?' countered Mansfield. 'I would never have thought a dry old stick like him would treat with the enemy behind our backs.'

'You can't call chatting casually in a bank treating with the enemy,' protested Auriole Allen.

'Lionel seemed to think it was. He sounded quite paranoid to me.'

'I don't understand,' she stammered. 'It's just not like Lionel. He's usually so – well, nice.'

'Emollient, you mean,' said the architect.

'Well...'

'To the Tower for us all, then,' said Mansfield astringently. 'Or into the arms of Calleford Construction, which is almost worse. Squeezing housing quarts into land pint pots is not for me and never will be.'

'I just don't believe Robert would do anything that harmed the firm.'

'Unless those rogues at Calleford Construction have bought him off,' said Mansfield. 'Had you thought of that? All I can say is that they haven't tried it on me. And just as well.'

'The trouble,' said Auriole Allen sadly, 'is that we've all got too much riding on Tolmie Park working out for Berebury Homes and we can't be certain that there's anywhere else to go. Calleford Construction's probably got all the staff it needs already – I know they've got a good young public relations manager – fully qualified, too.'

She looked up as Ned Phillips came round the corner of the corridor at speed, nearly bumping into the pair of them. 'Ah, there you are, Mrs Allen,' he said. 'You don't happen to know where Mr Selby is, do you? The accountants want a word with him but he's not in his office. Someone said he was in a crisis meeting somewhere but I don't know where and I can't find him anywhere.'

'"Out of this nettle, danger, we pluck this flower, safety,"' quoted Auriole Allen enigmatically. 'Or do we? Tell me that.'

'Tell me what, Mrs Allen?' asked Phillips.

'That everything in the garden is lovely.'

'Except that it isn't,' snapped Randolph Mansfield.

'The accountants didn't say anything about danger,' said Ned Phillips, cocking his head to one side interrogatively.

'No,' said Auriole dully. 'I don't suppose they did.'

'Accountants don't always know everything,' said Mansfield, ever the architect. 'They think they know everything but they don't. Take the value of good design, for instance. That costs more than they will ever believe.'

'I expect good design sells houses, though,' offered Ned Phillips brightly.

'Too right it does, Ned. That is, it ought to but you never can tell with the public.'

'At least you'll have the economies of scale at Tolmie,' said the young man.

'That's what Selby's always saying, isn't it?'

Ned Phillips grinned. 'All the time. Either everything goes according to plan at Tolmie Park or the firm should back off. Half cock and the scheme fails is what he says.'

Mansfield continued in a maritime metaphor. 'And it looks like what we've got is someone trying to scuttle the ship by opening the sea-cocks.'

A similar view was implicit in what was being said in the half-empty boardroom. Robert Selby had made no move to leave after Lionel Perry had strode out. He had been left with Derek Hitchin.

'And what was all that about, might I ask?' said the project officer.

'Your guess,' said the financial controller tautly, 'is as good as mine. All I did was pass the time of day with the fellow from Calleford Construction, although I must say I did wonder where the bank came in. They're our bankers as well as Calleford Construction's. And they're acting for this Stuart Bellamy who wants to buy us out, too. He referred us to Douglas Anderson there for any assurances about the validity of his offer and his capacity to come up with the money. It's all a bit worrying.'

'Sure,' said Hitchin half-heartedly.

'So is something else,' said Robert Selby, unusually forthcoming. 'We're very vulnerable to a take-over at this moment because we've got all this land at Tolmie. A good landbank is a very valuable commodity these days and you can bet your bottom dollar that Calleford Construction knows all about it. They couldn't have chosen a better moment to try to gobble us up. I suppose Stuart Bellamy knows that too.'

'A babe in arms could work it out,' said Derek Hitchin. 'We all know that land's the one thing that Calleford Construction always wants. They can't get enough of it especially now there's not enough to go round, anyway. Not now.'

Selby said, 'We all know that Calleford Construction is poised for a hostile takeover and I can tell you that the speed of response of the targeted company is what matters. It's critical to the outcome.'

Hitchin began to look interested. 'And Lionel's dragging his feet? That it? Or is he holding out for a better deal from this Bellamy fellow?'

The financial controller drummed his fingers on the table. 'Lionel could be playing a very deep game, of course. Very deep. With box car numbers, probably, because he hasn't asked for any recent ones from me.'

'Like chess, isn't it?' said Hitchin chattily.

'Except that we're all pawns,' said Selby, now sunk in gloom.

Derek Hitchin shrugged his shoulders. 'It's the knight's move that's always the surprise. It can go in any number of ways.'

'Not quite,' said Selby, taking this literally. He sat quite still and silent for a moment. Then he lifted his head and said half to himself, 'I wonder exactly what Lionel's playing at.'

Detective Inspector Sloan tilted his chair back on its hind legs, circled his hands round a large mug of coffee and said, 'Crosby, have you ever tried doing one of those puzzles where you are given some facts such as Tom is taller than Dick but not as tall as Harry so who is the shortest?'

'No, sir.'

'Or even,' he said reminiscently, taking another sip of coffee, 'one where you have water running into a bath at so many gallons a minute while it's running out through the plug-hole at another given rate and you have to work out how long it will take to overflow?'

'No, sir.'

'You're a lucky man.' Sloan set the mug down on his desk. 'You might even be said to have led a charmed life.'

'Why didn't they put the plug in, sir?'

'Exactly, Crosby. Why not?' Sloan pulled his notebook towards him and squinted down at his own handwriting. 'We are, you realise, faced with some similar problems but with one important exception.'

'Sir?'

'We don't have all the facts.'

'No, sir, but why did they want the bath to overflow anyway?'

'They didn't say,' responded Sloan gravely. 'Now today we have plenty of problems but not enough facts. Suppose, Crosby, for starters you list the problems. In date order, as they say when they haven't got a computer doing the hard work for them.'

Crosby frowned. 'The theft of the portrait?'

'Come, come, Crosby, the theft of the portrait was why we were called in. The action began well before that, with some person or persons unknown starting to look for the present Filligree of Tolmie. The woman at Arms and the Man told us it was a good month or more ago. Learning who that was is one of our problems.' He set his mug down. 'Only one of them, of course. Knowing why they wanted to find the man is another.'

'Then there was the theft of the portrait,' said Crosby doggedly.

'Preceded by the break-in,' said Sloan pensively. 'Incidentally, I'm not quite sure why the museum had to be broken into.'

'Because someone wanted the portrait,' said Crosby.

'I would have thought myself that taking the portrait while the museum was open would have been easier than breaking in.' said Sloan. 'After all, the portrait itself wasn't alarmed. All anyone had to do was wait until that gallery was empty, slit the painting round the edges, roll it up, and take it away.'

'Yes, sir.'

'What does that suggest to you?'

Crosby gave a prodigious frown but said nothing.

'To me,' said Sloan, 'it suggests that the thief or thieves were at work during the hours the museum was open.'

'Like Jonathon Ayling?'

'I think, Crosby, a search warrant is indicated there. I'm seeing the super next and then we can go.'

'Yes, sir.' Crosby's frown disappeared. 'So that was why it was overnight yesterday. Then early this morning the fire got started.'

'No, Crosby, before that – possibly also overnight – was the planting of the non-human bones on some very genuine lobster shells. That could have been done before or after the fire was set but as we don't know exactly when someone was last in the billiard room we can't put a date or time on it. Lobster shells don't grow on trees.'

Detective Constable Crosby didn't contest this statement. Instead he applied himself to his own mug of coffee. A muffled sound emerged from its depth. 'Nor do bones,' he said.

'True,' said Sloan. 'And Lionel Perry didn't know about the bones or the lobster shells. I'm sure about that. Shaken to the core, he was, when he heard about them. I find that very interesting, Crosby.'

'Yes, sir.' The detective constable sounded far from riveted. 'Then what?'

'Not a lot, you might say,' said Sloan, 'except an attempt at bribery and corruption – some might call it blackmail – and a little bit of arson. Not a lot of that either, mind you,' he added thoughtfully. 'Just enough to delay the development at Tolmie Park without jiggering it completely.'

Crosby brightened. 'Sir, is it to do with that thing they're always saying in court about time being of the essence?'

Detective Inspector Sloan set his mug back on his desk. 'You may have got something there, Crosby, but probably not in the way you think.'

'The Preservation Society must want as much time as they can get,' said Crosby, 'and Berebury Homes must want to get cracking on building as soon as they can.'

'Someone doesn't want them to, if what that planning man, Jeremy Stratton, says is true,' pointed out Sloan. 'They – whoever they are – said they were prepared to lay out good money in the cause.'

'I thought councils always held things up as long as they could anyway,' said Crosby. 'Surely they don't need bribing to do that.'

'For one so young, Crosby, you are very cynical.'

'Thank you, sir.'

'Which reminds me, Crosby, of someone else who is also prepared to lay out good money.'

'Sir?'

'If, Crosby, your employer instructed you to buy a property on his behalf no matter what it cost but the present owner didn't want to sell, what would be your next course of action?'

'To offer him a bit more,' said Crosby promptly.

'And if that didn't do the trick?'

'I'd report back to head office,' said Crosby, displaying a touching faith in those at police headquarters.

'And if you were then told that your job was on the line because you hadn't succeeded in getting the offer accepted?'

'I'd lean on the owner all over again.'

'You would, would you?' murmured Sloan.

'After all, if he was in it for the money, you'd think he'd sell in the end.'

'So you think Lionel Perry is only holding out for a better offer, do you?' said Sloan.

'Well, wouldn't you, sir?'

'Yes,' said Sloan thoughtfully, 'I think I would, but if that didn't work? What would you do then?'

'Then I'd smell a rat,' said the detective constable.

'I think, Crosby, you could be right. I'm beginning to get a distinct aroma of rattus rattus, deceased, too.' He said, 'And having smelt a rat, what then?'

The detective constable frowned. 'I think I would want to have a good look round for the rat.'

'Well done, Crosby. We need to know why there is a conflict of interest. After all, I suppose you could say that all crime amounts to a conflict of interest,' mused Sloan, putting this interesting thought aside for further consideration in a mythical future when he himself had more time. 'And why on earth should anyone be searching for the present Filligree of Tolmie now? Tell me that.'

'Dunno, sir.' The constable shook his head. 'Perhaps someone wants to steal his identity. Strikes me as a bit sinister, all the same. I hope we find him before they do, that's all.'

'Perhaps they needed his portrait to help find him,' mused Sloan.

'Or not let anyone else find him,' said Crosby. 'Had you thought of that, sir?'

Sloan stared at him.

CHAPTER SEVENTEEN

Stuart Bellamy had never kept the office hours considered sacrosanct – or even normal – by some. He didn't resent this, having long ago found that working for Jason Burke was more of a way of life than having an ordinary job. There were good reasons for this: the odd hours were important from Jason's business point of view. Some arrangers of gigs who were anxious for Kevin Cowlick to be with them on the night only came to life themselves after darkness had fallen, some were so crepuscular that if they were rung any earlier in the day they answered the telephone rubbing their eyes open. Neither cohort was as lucid as they would have been if they had been in contact later in the day. Disc jockeys were lucid all the same, which was nearly as bad.

And gigs and concert performances were the breath of life to Jason and his group as well as their bread and butter. Fixing these engagements up was only one of Stuart Bellamy's manifold duties. Another was listening to Jason riding one or other of his hobby horses. His leaping from an attack on the Health and Safety Acts to the purchase of Tolmie Park was in a manner that could be compared with a rider leaping bareback from one circus horse to another as they cantered round the ring. It usually caught Stuart Bellamy on the wrong foot.

'How are you getting on with that fellow from Berebury Homes?' he asked Bellamy, as he strummed a guitar in a leisurely way.

'I'm not,' said Bellamy shortly. Circumlocution was wasted on the back street boy from Luston. 'I've exactly nix to report, in fact, Jason. Whatever you say to him, Lionel Perry doesn't want to know and won't say why.'

'Funny that,' said Jason, one ear cocked towards his instrument as he picked out a tune on the guitar.

'Not even for funny money,' said Bellamy bitterly. 'In fact, funnily enough money doesn't seem to come into things.'

It was this aspect of his pursuit of Tolmie Park that immediately engaged Jason Burke's attention. 'Doesn't make sense to me. You'd better find out why not, then, hadn't you?' said Jason.

'Like how?' asked Bellamy.

'Your problem, mate, not mine.'

Stuart Bellamy sighed. Long ago someone had instilled into the young Jason Burke the importance of not shouldering other people's burdens and he had learnt the lesson well. As far as his manager was concerned even getting Jason to shoulder his own problems would have been something.

'So go get it sorted,' said Jason. He hitched himself upright. 'Hey, before you go, let's just have a listen to this new disc that's just come in. I think it's worth an ear.'

So it was therefore quite late and quite dark by the time Stuart Bellamy left Jason Burke's house and made his way back to Acacia Avenue and his home.

He knew that something was wrong before he had done little more than put his key in the lock in the front door.

Fumbling for the light switch in the entrance hall, he found that no light resulted from his touch.

Cursing at a spent lightbulb he advanced towards a light switch in another room.

Well before he reached the next light switch he stumbled over something on the floor and fell forwards, conscious of a figure brushing past him in the darkness and out of the front door as he did so. Then all he was aware of was the sound of the door being shut behind him as someone left the house.

And minutes later he was treated to the sight of a house reduced to chaos.

Wendy Pullen looked round her sitting room, once more packed with members of the Berebury Preservation Society. 'We've been overtaken by events,' she declaimed dramatically. 'There's nothing more we should be doing to save Tolmie Park for the time being. Nothing, Jonathon, do you understand?'

'Yes, Wendy,' he said meekly. This meeting had been called for soon after he had left work.

'Not now.'

'No, Wendy.'

'If the police are involved then there's no need for us any more.' Wendy Pullen had once been recorded on video camera by the constabulary when leading a protest march and had never felt the same way again about those guardians of the peace. 'Our hands are tied.'

'As long as none of us had any hand in the arson, that is,' added Paul Pullen with his customary exactitude. 'Or the theft of the oil painting.'

'If we didn't,' observed a more percipient member of the group, 'then it means that someone else also has an interest in stopping the development.'

'Or accelerating it,' said another speaker, 'if they were hoping the whole place would burn down.'

'Vested interest, either way,' said a woman in the front row. The speaker, who lived very well on her unearned income, was touchingly naive about how this income was achieved.

Paul Pullen quoted an old saw. 'Hell hath no fury like a vested interest masquerading as a principle.'

'Yes – well,' said Wendy, 'I don't think we need to go into any of this just now. Not our problem.'

'Not our problem.' Paul Pullen firmly endorsed this. He spent a lot of his time trying to keep his wife from picking up problems that were not hers. The Berebury Preservation Society was one of the safer areas into which he had been able to channel her energies. At least it had been safe until now.

'There's just one thing,' said Jonathon Ayling. 'The police have interviewed me and warned me that I may be charged with breaking and entering.'

Wendy Pullen bristled. 'Why?'

'It was because of my shoes.' There was a mock solemnity about his answer.

'Your shoes?'

He nodded. 'My shoes. They found little shards of glass in them...'

'What's that got to do with...?'

'...that matches the glass in the broken window in the Greatorex Museum.'

The room fell silent. Then Wendy said grimly, 'Jonathon, what have you been up to?'

'Trying to save Tolmie Park,' he said. 'That's what you all wanted, wasn't it?'

'Call coming in from Stuart Bellamy, sir,' said Detective Constable Crosby, handing over the telephone. 'He's just got home from work and found a burglar in the house. At least he thinks it was a burglar. He sounds pretty upset to me.'

Sloan took the receiver and waited. Nothing about this case would surprise him now. Nothing.

'Absolute chaos, Inspector,' insisted Stuart Bellamy. 'It's absolute chaos here.'

'Go on,' said Sloan evenly.

'I must have disturbed him, whoever he was, when I opened the door. He scooted off pretty quickly I can tell you. Thank goodness,' he added as an afterthought.

'Yes,' agreed Sloan soberly. Tackling burglars was not for your amateur. Any policeman would say that. 'Anything taken?'

'Who knows?' wailed Bellamy. 'The whole place has been turned over. It's a complete tip. What my wife will say when she gets back from her mother's I daren't begin to think. I'll be a dead man and she'll go bananas. Do you know, he's even ripped all the cushions open. What do you make of that?'

'I would say that your intruder was looking for something,' said Sloan, unsurprised, making a note to send a scene of crime officer around as soon as possible.

'But what?' asked Bellamy hoarsely.

'I can't answer that,' said Sloan, asking pertinently, 'can you?'

'Me? How should I know what a burglar wanted? I – we – don't have anything particularly valuable. My wife likes that Moorcroft pottery – but that hasn't been touched.'

Somehow Detective Inspector Sloan did not think that some Moorcroft vases had been what the thief had been seeking. 'But,' he concluded aloud, 'we can't tell yet whether or not he found what it was he was looking for.'

'But why should he want anything at all that we've got in our house?' asked Bellamy.

'I can't answer that question either.' Detective Inspector Sloan was beginning to think he could make a sporting guess at it but he did not say so. There was just the one item that he knew of that had gone missing that day.

A portrait of Sir Francis Filligree, fourth baronet, taken from the Greatorex Museum.

It was only after he'd rung off that Sloan remembered the Anglo-Saxon artefacts that had gone missing today, too.

CHAPTER EIGHTEEN

Minutes later Sloan was reporting to Superintendent Leeyes.

'So we have to add attempted burglary to today's activities, do we, Sloan?'

'It looks very much like it, sir.'

'It seems to me, Sloan, as if a thorough grounding in mid-sixteenth century Italian politics would have been a help to you today.' Superintendent Leeyes was a lifelong admirer of Niccolò Machiavelli. 'In my experience that's what you need when local authorities come into things and as for pop stars...' He rolled his eyes in a gesture of despair.

'Jeremy Stratton, their planning officer, did report the attempted bribe to us, sir,' ventured Sloan.

'Only when he was threatened by exposure,' pointed out Leeyes.

'He still needn't have done.'

'But there's no evidence anywhere for either, is there?' said Leeyes irritably. 'No independent witnesses, for instance. He could have made the whole thing up.'

'In that case,' persisted Sloan, 'we would need to be asking ourselves why he did. Knowing even that could be just as important.'

Superintendent Leeyes blew out his cheeks and pronounced

something that had been a lifelong maxim in his own working life. 'When in doubt, Sloan, confuse the issue. That's what they might have been doing. All of 'em.'

Sloan didn't know whether this sentiment had come from Machiavelli: it could well have done. 'I don't think matters could be more confused than they are at the moment,' he admitted. Attempted burglary, attempted bribery, definite arson, confirmed burglary all contributed to a melange of broken laws that he could well have done without. And that didn't include anything that lunatic Jonathon Ayling had in mind.

'Don't count on it, Sloan, that's all. That light at the end of the tunnel could well be a train coming the other way.'

'Yes, sir, I'm sure.' With the superintendent there was always too much hope about. 'The only thing that seems quite clear at the present moment is that some person or persons unknown want to delay the start of the development at Tolmie Park for reasons that are not immediately obvious to us.'

Leeyes grunted.

'And that either the same people or others are looking for the present members of the family of Filligree of Tolmie.'

'Then we shouldn't be surprised at there being backhanders about, should we, Sloan?'

'No, sir,' he said. The superintendent had never been surprised at the suggestion of backhanders anywhere – everywhere.

'What isn't at all clear,' Leeyes rumbled on, 'is where the theft of the portrait comes into the development question. If it does.'

'In connection with which, sir, we're just going to execute a search warrant at Jonathon Ayling's house.' Perhaps Crosby had been right about someone not wanting the portrait found. Perhaps it was what had been taken from Stuart Bellamy's house. If something had been.

'About time, too,' grunted Leeyes.

'And we've now had some feedback from Companies House,' said Sloan, picking up a message sheet. 'Lionel Perry is the biggest shareholder in Berebury Homes. His wife has a substantial holding, too…'

'That's a lot of family eggs in one basket,' observed Leeyes.

'And so has Robert Selby – he's their finance man.'

'Putting his money where is mouth is?'

'Only in a manner of speaking, sir.' Sloan countered phrase with fable. 'He might just have worked out on which side his bread is buttered and he of all people – being in finance, that is – should be in a position to know.'

'Or,' said Leeyes trenchantly, 'he might know something that we don't.'

'All our thoughts on that are still open.' Detective Inspector Sloan turned back a few pages of his notebook. 'Nobody else in the top echelons of the firm seems to have more than a token holding.'

'Eggs in other baskets, I suppose.'

'Or no eggs,' said Sloan. He bent his head over his notebook again.

'Or not wanting to put them in the firm's basket,' said Leeyes.

'I can only say that the two things that seem to have really upset Lionel Perry so far are the bones and the lobster shells.'

'Not the fire?'

'No, but I swear he didn't know about either the bones or the lobster shells until I told him and that shook him.'

'These lobster shells, Sloan,' Leeyes frowned. 'What do you make of them?'

'A shot over someone's bows but who it's meant as a warning for, I don't know. And what about, I don't know either.'

'Then find out, Sloan,' said the superintendent testily, 'and soon.'

After he'd clambered into the passenger seat of the police car Detective Inspector Sloan allowed himself the luxury of a yawn. 'It's been a long day, Crosby. We should be able to knock off after this and get some proper food.'

Detective Constable Crosby, thus encouraged, notched up the speed of the police car.

'Jonathon Ayling should be back home after work by now. After we've searched his place we can all go home.'

Jonathon Ayling was indeed at home.

And strangely indifferent to the production of a search warrant.

'Too late,' he said dully.

'Nevertheless…' began Sloan.

'Come this way.' He led the two policemen round the back of the house and pointed to a small window. It had obviously been forced and now dangled drunkenly on a broken hinge. 'Breaking and entering.'

'Sauce for the goose, sauce for the gander,' muttered Crosby.

'Anything taken?' asked Sloan, who had known stolen

goods go missing again and again, especially when being sought by their rightful owners.

'Like a portrait?' said Crosby under his breath.

'I've never seen anything like it,' said Ayling, still stunned. 'It's absolute mayhem indoors. It looks as if I only just missed him.'

The house, Sloan could only agree, was in a poor state. Every drawer had been emptied onto the floor and upstairs in the bedroom, the mattress overturned and the wardrobe ransacked. Just like Stuart Bellamy had reported only a little earlier.

'What do you suppose someone was looking for?' asked Sloan.

Jonathon Ayling didn't answer him. All he did was stare at a room turned upside down.

'And have they found it?' asked Sloan.

'I couldn't say,' responded Ayling stiffly.

'I think you can,' said Sloan.

There was an uneasy silence

'You see,' went on Sloan in a conversational tone, 'if the portrait of Sir Francis Filligree has been stolen from here it can only be for one reason.'

Jonathon Ayling still did not speak.

'And that,' said Sloan implacably, 'is because someone might be able to recognise a current member of the Filligree family from it.'

Ayling sank onto a bedside chair, head in hands. 'I know. That's what he said.'

'Who?'

'The guy who wanted it stolen – well, taken, anyway.'

'Theft is theft,' chanted Crosby sententiously.

'This fellow said in this case it wasn't theft.'

'Who?' asked Sloan again.

'The one I met in the pub. The Claviger's Arms over at Almstone.'

'Go on.'

'I was talking about what we were going to do about the development at Tolmie – I'd had a few by then – well, quite a few, actually – and this guy who was there asked what. I told him I thought if a few Anglo-Saxon bits and pieces were to be discovered there, that it would hold things up a bit.'

'It would,' agreed Sloan. He'd learnt that much about planning today. 'Go on.'

'He thought that sounded a great idea.' Jonathon Ayling said 'I did, too. After all, they'd be taken straight back from whence they came. Bound to be. And it wasn't as if they were anything in themselves.'

Detective Constable Crosby gave a low growl. The unimportance of the intrinsic value of stolen goods had been the subject of one of the lectures he'd had to attend.

'Go on,' commanded Sloan.

'He asked where I was going to get them and I said the museum and he said well if I was going to do that, would I take the portrait as well – just to have it kept safe. He was going to give it back later, no questions asked.'

'Oh, he was, was he?' began Crosby.

'Who was he?' barked Sloan.

'Didn't give me his name – just his mobile phone number. He didn't want the portrait himself – I was just to keep it safe and then give it back when he said. It's well and truly gone now, all right.'

'What did he look like?' asked Sloan, an eye, as always, on the essentials.

'Can't say that I took a lot of notice at the time. You know how dark it is in these really old pubs and anyway I was pretty plastered by then.'

'Never mind that,' said Sloan. 'Give me his mobile number as quickly as you can.'

Jonathon Ayling handed it over and then there was an uneasy silence as it became clear that the mobile telephone was not going to be answered.

'There was one thing about him – the man in the pub – that I do remember,' offered Ayling. 'He was ginger-haired.'

'Come on, Crosby,' snapped Sloan, tossing the telephone back to Ayling. 'We haven't got time to hang about.'

'Yes, sir. I mean, no sir. Where to?'

'Wherever it was Ned Phillips said he lived. You've got the address in your notebook. Quickly, now.'

'Almstone village,' said Crosby, flicking through his notebook at speed. 'I'm sure I've got Ned Phillips down as living in Almstone. Yes, here it is.'

'You'd better be sure,' said Sloan grimly, as they scampered for the car in the manner of drivers at start of the old Le Mans race. He reached for the microphone before he'd even slammed the car door shut, calling up police headquarters as Crosby started up the car.

'Attention, attention,' said Sloan as Crosby slammed his way swiftly up the car's gears. 'Any car within reach of

Almstone village to attend One Five – Fifteen – High Street, Almstone, and ensure personal safety of a man going under the name of Ned Phillips. Over.'

The crisp impersonal tones of the Controller came in response. 'Message received, caller. Please identify your position.'

'Between Larking and Tolmie,' said Crosby.

'Oh Lord,' said Sloan.

'What was that, caller?'

'About seven miles south of Almstone on the Larking road,' said Sloan.

The microphone came to life again. 'Two cars attending from Calleford, caller.'

'That's miles away from Almstone,' groaned Sloan.

'Their ETA not yet known.'

'They'll be too late,' said Sloan.

'And one on its way from Luston,' said the voice over the air.

'That's farther away still.'

'Further information on the nature of the emergency required, caller. Is it a domestic?'

'No,' Sloan said into the microphone. 'Not a domestic. A serious attack possibly imminent.' That was the trouble with today, he thought. People were beginning to think that only husbands and wives hit each other. Personal safety wasn't only about battered husbands and wives.

The controller was obviously thinking along other, different, lines. 'Are body armour and firearms likely to be needed?'

'It's too early to say.' Sloan cast a sidelong glance at Crosby and said, 'or too late.'

'Six miles,' said Crosby. 'There's Billing Bridge, though.'
Billing Bridge had been the way over the River Alm since
medieval times. It had been built wide enough to take a horse
driven wooden cart, not two fast cars travelling in opposite
directions, one at least travelling at a speed not allowed on
any road in the country. As traffic hold-ups went, on a busy
day it was in a class of its own.

Sloan was still talking to the controller at police
headquarters. 'Locate and detain for questioning the
following staff of Berebury Homes: Lionel Perry, Robert
Selby, Randolph Mansfield and Ned Phillips – if you can find
him.'

'Five miles,' sang out Crosby.

Sloan was still talking into the microphone. 'Notify me of
anyone who can't be found,' he said. For reasons too complex
to quantify he had left Auriole Allen off his list.

'Noted, caller,' came cool tones from some distant control
room. The speaker there wasn't being bounced about in a
speeding car, blue light flashing, police siren sounding out
across the empty fields.

'And tell me if you get a three nines call from Almstone,'
added Sloan for good measure. Chance, he thought, would be
a fine thing.

'Requests logged, caller,' said the same dispassionate voice.

Detective Inspector Sloan leant back – in complete contrast
with Detective Constable Crosby who was crouched over the
wheel as if he could coax another few miles an hour out of the
car by leaning forward. With a Herculean effort, Sloan took
his eyes off the road and thought about where they were going
and what they might find. They had 'At Risk' registers for

children in bad homes but they didn't have one at all for a ginger-haired man tangling with a desperate one.

'Billing Bridge coming up,' said Crosby, putting his foot down even further when he caught sight of another car approaching the bridge from the opposite side of the river.

'I'll book him if he doesn't stop,' vowed Crosby.

As if he had read the constable's lips, the other driver fell back on his side of the bridge leaving the police car a clear run. Sloan was conscious of the police car picking up speed once safely over the river but only at one level of his awareness. The rest of his mind was engaged in thinking of what might lie ahead.

'Three and a half miles,' chanted Crosby.

Sloan called up control again. 'Get someone to check the Claviger's Arms at Almstone. Ned Phillips might be there.'

'Message received.' The controller sounded distant and detached – rather like the cows present near Bosworth Field who would have observed the end of the Plantagenets with bovine indifference.

While the police car passed fields and hedges at speed Sloan had another thought. He bent towards the microphone yet again. 'Get someone in C Division to start checking on the senior staff at Calleford Construction, too.' That was something he hadn't got round to yet.

'Message received.'

'And locate but do not detain Jason Burke and Stuart Bellamy.'

'Message received.'

'Just over two miles to go, sir,' said Crosby.

Sloan cast another sidelong glance at him. The detective

constable was concentrating on the road with the close attention that he never gave to his notebook. His only moment of indecision came when he spotted an oncoming car approaching a crossroads with the clear – and duly signalled – intention of turning right ahead of the police car. Crosby put his foot down and the car leapt forward into the rapidly closing gap. When Sloan opened his eyes again there was no sign of either the other car or the crossroads.

'Not far to go now, sir,' said the constable serenely. 'Almstone's just round the corner now.'

He brought the police car to a halt outside a modest cottage and the two men tumbled out.

'You take the front, Crosby,' said Sloan, 'and I'll go round the back.'

It was just as well he did. The kitchen door was ajar. Inside, Lionel Perry, knife in hand, already had Ned Phillips pinned down in his chair, blood everywhere. Gone was the face of the urbane company chairman: instead there was a visage contorted by anger and desperation.

His hand was raised to take another lunge at the sitting man when Detective Inspector Sloan gripped his wrist so hard that, giving a squeal of pain, Perry dropped the knife to the floor.

CHAPTER NINETEEN

By the time the doctors allowed the police to interview Ned Phillips the next morning the young man was sitting, stitched and bandaged, in a hospital bed. He was more than ready to tell his story.

'He nearly got me,' he said hoarsely, still surprised at the narrowness of his escape. 'I wasn't expecting him, you see. He just came in the back door behind me as I was sitting down having my supper in the kitchen.'

'You were very lucky,' said Sloan soberly. 'Stab wounds are always more serious than they look.' That was another lesson you learnt early on the beat.

Ned Phillips managed a grin. 'That's what the doctors said. He must have hit my shoulder blade the first time. He'd have got me properly with his next effort if you hadn't got there.'

'Too right he would,' said Detective Constable Crosby, never one for false modesty.

'I never thought he'd ever do something like that,' admitted Ned Phillips. 'I thought it was all a bit of a lark.'

'Lionel Perry didn't,' said Sloan. 'He was at his wits' end.'

'What I want to know is why did he go for me just then?' said Phillips. 'He'd been seeing me around for quite a while.'

'That's easily explained.' said Sloan. 'Until today he'd been seeing you without knowing who you were.'

Ned Phillips frowned. 'So how did he get to know I was me, so to speak?'

Sloan said, 'As soon as he got his hands on the portrait of Sir Francis.'

Ned Phillips groaned. 'That's what worried me. You see, everyone has always said I was the spitting image of my sainted ancestor. But how did he know where to find the portrait?'

Sloan said 'That's easy. The firm's press officer, Mrs Allen, mentioned at a meeting that the newspaper reporter had told her about the stolen portrait and that they'd had a tip-off that the police were chasing a couple of likely suspects. One way and another Bellamy and Ayling had both been involved with Tolmie Park.' Sloan's interview with Auriole Allen had been a painful mix of guilt and disillusion. Nobody likes to learn that the firm's boss to whom for so long one had been unfailingly loyal had had not so much clay feet as clay legs.

'Beats me how the paper gets to know these things before anyone else,' muttered Crosby.

'They have ways and means not open to the Force,' said Sloan. This was a sore subject in some quarters: it gave the press leverage when trying to act as judge and jury. 'That was when Perry put two and two together. Luckily he searched Bellamy's house before he went to Jonathon Ayling's place.'

Phillips groaned again. 'Ayling was so sure it would be safe in his house.'

'Well, it wasn't, was it?' said Crosby flatly.

'Lionel Perry had been looking for us everywhere...' said Phillips.

'Us?' interrupted Sloan.

'The family,' said Ned Phillips. 'He put an enquiry agent on to it but he couldn't find us in England because we weren't there.'

'You were in Switzerland, weren't you?' said Sloan. At a guess, Lionel Perry had gone out there, too, snapping famous mountains as he went. One of the well-known ways of disguising something was to stress it: everyone would know he went there on his holidays.

Phillips nodded, promptly discovered that this action was painful and so stilled his head. 'The family never came back after grandfather died there in the war. My mother's Swiss, you see, and they don't use the title now.'

'He didn't dare advertise for you for fear everyone would wonder why,' said Sloan.

'Anyway,' said Ned Phillips, 'when Dad heard that someone had been sniffing around I offered to come over and see what all the fuss was about.'

'The Muster Green,' supplied Detective Inspector Sloan. Derek Hitchin had remembered how Lionel Perry had suggested developing that separately but the thought that Berebury Homes might not have owned it had come from the architect, Randolph Mansfield. 'Lionel must have taken a really close look at the title deeds and seen they didn't include it.'

'The Muster Green,' agreed Ned Phillips. He leant back on his pillow, winced and sat up again rather quickly. 'You see that was never included in the sale of the property because it had been used by the militia for yonks – including grandfather and his beloved Territorials – without the Filligrees ever charging anyone for it. The civil defence people were still training there in the cold war or something...' he added, dismissing a serious blip in European history with all the insouciance of youth. 'And anyway, Dad wanted to keep a bit of old England because it had mattered so much to grandfather before the White Plague got him.'

'A foothold,' said Crosby, unaware that that word, too, had a military meaning.

'But Lionel didn't know that,' said Sloan, 'until later.'

'I don't suppose anyone did,' said Ned Phillips cheerfully. 'Unless they checked. From a landscape point of view it looks as if it belongs because it always did. It would have been easy for everyone to assume that the Muster Green was part of the whole especially as no one else had been near it for over sixty years.'

'Neither part nor parcel,' said Sloan. That had been the trouble.

'Berebury Homes were taking on lots of extra staff to cope with the new development there,' said Ned, 'so I applied, too. I'd been educated over here so no one guessed.' He pulled his lips down in mock grimace. 'Robert Selby's not such a bad old stick really.'

It was Robert Selby who'd been up most of the night calculating the financial importance to Berebury Homes of not owning the Muster Green.

Ned Phillips couldn't stop talking. 'Then, of course, being around in the firm I got to hear that the Berebury Preservation Society wanted to delay building so I set out to find their Jonathon Ayling and got him to collect the portrait from the museum while he was about it...'

'Collect?' said Crosby indignantly. 'Steal, you mean.'

'And while he was about what?' asked Sloan, policeman first, last and all the time.

'The portrait was only on loan to the museum,' said Ned. 'My father told me that.'

Crosby subsided, rumbling. Sloan pulled his notebook a little nearer.

Phillips carried on. 'Ayling needn't have bothered nicking his Anglo-Saxon bits and pieces to plant in the ground because delay was all that Lionel Perry wanted, too. We didn't know that at the time, of course.'

'The fire,' said Crosby suddenly.

'I guess that was our Lionel,' said Ned Phillips.

'But why the bones and the lobster shells?' asked Sloan. It had always been obvious that the fire was merely to slow things down, not do lasting damage.

Phillips managed a half-smile. 'That was me. Lionel did his dirty work in the billiard room through a broken window and can't have seen them. I borrowed a key. Easy. It was just to let Lionel know that there was a Filligree around. A sort of shot across the bows.'

'It frightened him,' agreed Sloan. In his experience frightened men did things that confident men never would.

'And he frightened me,' admitted Ned Phillips, closing his eyes and visibly tired.

'Lionel Perry made a big mistake,' said Detective Inspector Sloan.

'Criminals usually do,' said Superintendent Leeyes loftily. 'What put you on to it?'

'Something Crosby said.' Sloan believed in giving credit where credit was due.

'Crosby?' The superintendent's eyebrows almost disappeared. 'Are you sure?'

'He pointed out that the portrait might have been stolen – taken – from the museum not to help find Phillips but to stop anyone else finding him. You see, sir, Lionel Perry thought that Ned Phillips was the only one besides himself who knew about the true ownership of the land that Berebury Homes needed so badly – he didn't know the fellow's father was alive and well, too.'

'Hadn't done his homework, had he?' said Leeyes.

'He'd tried to find out but he hadn't been able to find the family anywhere and then when he realised that Ned had found him first, he knew the young man could have him over a barrel.'

'So in effect Phillips owned a ransom strip,' mused Leeyes. 'Nice work, if you can get it.'

'It's been done before,' murmured Sloan. It was called leverage but there were uglier names for the practice. 'Time and again, I would say.'

'There are other ways of keeping people quiet,' said Leeyes.

Detective Inspector Sloan said, 'I don't think Ned Phillips was going to keep quiet, no matter what. But the real danger was from somewhere else entirely.'

'Are you going to tell me, Sloan, or do I have to ask?'

'All the while the project was delayed Lionel Perry could keep quiet about the Muster Green and hope to come to terms with the real owner when he found him. After all, you don't need to own land to put in for permission to build on it.'

Sloan had just had a crash course in planning law from Jeremy Stratton at the council offices. Why he should have cited the London Fire Acts of 1701 as splendid examples of good planning law Sloan still wasn't quite sure, except that they, too, had concerned burning buildings.

'And?'

'And then Calleford Construction came on the scene looking for a takeover. Their Due Diligence team would have spotted the discrepancy straightaway and with Ned Phillips around Lionel would have had no chance of talking his way out of it or pleading adverse possession...' Sloan caught sight of his superior officer's expression and added hastily, 'As you know, sir, that means that people who have been occupying it for so many years without challenge can claim it as theirs.'

'That sounds a most unsatisfactory procedure,' said Leeyes, momentarily diverted and condemning it out of hand.

'Lionel Perry's personal stake in Berebury Homes would have lost a lot of value the minute Calleford Construction found his firm didn't own the Muster Green after all.'

He didn't want to go into the ethics of adverse possession. Not with knowing what he did about the superintendent's views on squatters.

'So why didn't he sell out to that singer person?' The superintendent couldn't bring himself to use Jason Burke's professional name and the words Kevin Cowlick were destined never to cross his lips.

'Because Burke's solicitors would have spotted the discrepancy in the same way Calleford Construction's would have done, and without proper access Perry would have had to sell the land at a loss. Hs only hope was to forge ahead and hope he could either get away with it or silence the present owner of the Muster Green.'

'I said all along that money came into this somewhere, Sloan,' said Leeyes grandly.

'So you did, sir,' said Sloan, sycophancy being nearly as good as flattery in getting you anywhere.

CHAPTER TWENTY

That money came into the situation had never been in doubt at the offices of Berebury Homes Ltd.

Robert Selby was taking the lead and being long-winded about it into the bargain. 'I may be being over-optimistic but I think the danger of a takeover from Calleford Construction may have receded somewhat.'

There was a chorus of reassurance.

'They're not going to touch us with a bargepole if there's a criminal case in the offing,' said Derek Hitchin. 'That sort of aggro spells nothing but trouble to an outfit like theirs. They've always been people in it for a quick kill and this pretty kettle of fish'll all take an age to sort out.'

'I don't think that their architect would be able to draw up a scheme without using the Muster Green access any more than I could,' put in Randolph Mansfield, frowning.

Auriole Allen said, 'Tell me, folks, if I've got this all wrong but if they couldn't do it, how could we?'

'Lionel was counting on our not needing to,' said Mansfield.

Robert Selby allowed a thin smile to play along his lips. 'They let me into the hospital to see young Ned Phillips this afternoon – Edward Filligree, I suppose I should call him now.'

'I heard he was out of danger,' said Auriole Allen, adding automatically, 'I've sent a card and flowers.'

'So has Jason Burke,' said Selby. 'I'm afraid Calleford Construction is not the only interested party.'

'Go on,' said Derek Hitchin, his eyes still on the financial controller.

'I raised with him the possibility of a management buyout in certain circumstances – certain favourable circumstances, of course,' said Selby.

'Without Lionel, you mean?' said Randolph Mansfield.

'Without either Lionel or Calleford Construction.' The financial controller let the sentence hang in the air before he said, 'Ned seemed quite interested in coming in with us if we make a bid for it. Said he'd seen the books, anyway, while he was working for me.'

Hitchin slapped his thigh. 'Bringing the Muster Green with him, of course. I like it.'

'What he said to me,' said Robert Selby, staid as always, 'was that the Filligrees of Tolmie had always had a gambling streak but he didn't know if his father would be willing to follow in the family tradition and take a punt on it.' He paused and then said, 'Or whether his father would want to take Jason Burke's money and run. He said we'd just have to wait and see.'

OTHER TITLES BY CATHERINE AIRD

AVAILABLE FROM

ALLISON & BUSBY

☐ *Hole in One*   978-0-7490-8292-5   £6.99

All Allison & Busby titles can be ordered from our website,
www.allisonandbusby.com,
or from your local bookshop and are also
available by post from:

Bookpost, PO Box 29, Douglas, Isle of Man, IM99 1BQ
Credit cards accepted. For details:
Telephone: +44(0)1624 677237
Fax: +44(0)1624 670923
Email: bookshop@enterprise.net
www.bookpost.co.uk

Free postage and packing in the United Kingdom.